Flower Frenzy

A PRIDE STREET PARANORMAL COZY MYSTERY
BOOK TWO

T. THORN COYLE

CHAPTER 1

Marsha

IT WAS THAT HUMANS-WAKE-UP-LATE DAY, and Klaus was rattling our empty food bowls in the big, bright kitchen. I had just come in from doing my morning business in the back garden—thank goodness for the kitchen doggie door!—and was hungry myself.

"Why do they do this?" Klaus complained. His bark was more of a whine. I couldn't really blame him. Sundays were annoying. The house was too quiet. The kitchen with its gleaming white countertops, and the island where our food bowls were was clean and tidy, just the way John and Garrett liked it. And, most importantly, the doors of the navy-blue cupboard where our food and treats were stored remained firmly closed.

Our food used to be stored in a cute canister on the island shelf, next to our food and water dishes, until I figured out how to knock it down and paw the cover off. After that? Our treats moved to a high cupboard my little legs couldn't reach, even when I stood on my hind legs.

Believe me, I tried. Many times.

Klaus nosed the metal bowl, again, rattling it in its cunning holder cut into the island shelf.

A tan and white corgi, Klaus is younger than me. He's my best friend, though I'm not about to tell him that. He's soppy enough as it is. Klaus is also not nearly as beautiful and smart as I am, but I suppose that's not his fault. We can't help that some of us are born with glossy black coats and brown and white makeup and others of us are not.

As for the smarts, what can I say? My brain is as complex as my nose. And right now, my nose was not smelling any breakfast. And my ears didn't pick up on any sounds from upstairs, which was even more worrying.

I glanced at the door into the dining room where Adam the ghost leaned, his leather cap set at a jaunty angle on his head, bare arms crossed to show off his chest to full advantage under his leather vest. His black boots gleamed softly in the morning sun streaming through the window above the big white sink.

Considering that most of the light streamed right through him, the fact that his boots gleamed at all was a testament to how shiny and well-polished they were. At least I couldn't smell them. The smell of boot polish makes me want to bite something, and I really did not want to bite Adam. Ever.

It's bad enough when he scratches my head. His hands are icy cold and go right through me, which, let me tell you, is very, very weird.

This was Adam's home when he was alive. Klaus had found a box of his stuff in the crawlspace behind the big closet we're not supposed to go into. Too many temptations, John likes to say. John hates it when we chew his shoes and steal his feather boas. But I ask you, what else are shoes and boas for?

Adam likes leather even more than Klaus and I do, but as far as I know, he doesn't chew it. Though his teeth look like they might sink into a nice shoe if they really wanted to.

::They were up late last night,:: Adam said.

Didn't I know it? They had disturbed my sleep, coming in from who knows where? A corgi needs her sleep.

"Go get them, Marsha!" Klaus whined.

"Why me?"

Klaus turned his fuzzy little head away, the stinker. I sighed. Why did the responsibility always fall on me? Neither of us liked going up and down the big staircase, even after Garrett had put down the carpet runner. At least now our toenails had something to grab, but that didn't make climbing the stairs—and worse, coming down head first!—any less of a chore.

::They're up,:: Adam said, tilting his chin upstairs.

"Goodie, goodie, goodie!" Klaus banged his bowl one last time, then started prancing excitedly.

I barked a greeting. *"Good morning, humans! It's breakfast time!"*

"Break-fast! Break-fast!" Klaus barked, chasing me around the island.

"All right, you two!" John said, entering the kitchen in bare feet, soft gray pants, and a white t-shirt. His black hair stuck up straight on one side, and his dark eyes looked a bit tired.

He didn't even notice Adam, who moved quickly out of the way.

Garrett shuffled in behind him, seal brown hair flopping over his glasses, his pale skin looking a bit puffy. Sometimes when humans had a good time, they looked terrible the next morning. Guess last night was really fun.

He wore a long soft robe that I loved to curl up on. Garrett blinked at the sunlight, then yawned and headed to the sink as Klaus and I danced around John's feet, waiting for him to get our food down. Mornings we got a small scoop of wet food each, and a common bowl of kibble.

"Wet. Food! Wet. Food!" Klaus barked.

Garrett filled the coffee pot, and John set our water dish in the sink then got out the can opener. I looked back at the dining room door. Adam had disappeared.

Sometimes he stayed to watch Garrett and John, with a strange look on his face. I think he missed being alive. At least John and Garrett had started noticing when Klaus and I interacted with the ghost. They talked to him sometimes. Plus, Adam helped us all solve the case of the poisoned waiter. That really made Garrett pay attention.

"Here you go, you demanding little queens," John said, setting our wet food bowls into their rightful slots on the island shelf.

"Not a queen!" Klaus barked. *"I'm a corgi!"*

I didn't bother answering, just stuck my snoot into my bowl and started snarfing down.

John patted my back, then padded over to Garrett. I smelled the yummy coffee smells. We weren't allowed to drink coffee, but sometimes coffee came with sweets and treats, and sometimes Garrett dropped something. John never dropped his food, but Garrett was a little clumsier. Just like Klaus.

"Breakfast here?" John asked Garrett, "or do you want to go to Bruisers?"

"Bruisers!" Klaus woofed around a mouthful of food.

"You're disgusting," I replied. *"Don't talk with your mouth full, you almost sprayed wet food on me that time."*

I mean, I love Klaus and all, but sometimes he is so annoying.

Klaus ignored me, and we both went back to our food, though I kept one ear swiveled toward the conversation at the gurgling coffee percolator.

"It's such a pretty day," Garrett said, "why don't we walk to Bruiser's before I head to work? And that way, I don't have to clean up the kitchen after you cook!"

John laughed and swatted Garrett's butt. Garrett gave him a smooch, then took his mug and headed back upstairs with a swirl of his robe.

"How about it, you two? Want to go visit your friend?"

I licked the last bit of food from my chops, then looked up at him and smiled.

"I'll take that as a yes," he said. "Okay, I'm going to make my ancestor offerings, then get changed. I'll give you your kibble when we get back, okay?"

Klaus barked an affirmative, and John headed into the dining room where a little shrine hung on the wall.

As I lapped up water, I heard the snick of a lighter and smelled incense.

John honored his ancestors every day, and I knew they were important to him. I guess ancestors were a lot like ghosts, even though I'd never seen them.

I felt a cold draught in the kitchen again. Adam was back, that wistful look on his face again. He looked at me, then walked into the dining room.

It made me wonder, did anyone ever light incense for Adam? Or had all his friends forgotten he was once alive?

I trotted into the dining room, and there he was, leaning against the wall near the big, wood-framed windows, watching John place the incense into the small holder on the hanging wall altar next to the orange that sat in front of a series of small photographs.

"Adam needs a photo!" I barked at John's back.

He bowed to the altar, then turned.

"What's that, Marsha P. Johnson?" He crouched and held out a hand.

"Adam! We need to pay more attention to Adam!"

::*That's okay, I don't need anything,*:: the ghost replied, then winked out again. But his voice sounded sad to me.

"That's right! We're going for a walk!" John said, standing up again. "Just let me get some clothes on and brush my hair."

Klaus clicked into the dining room.

"What's happening?" he asked.

I looked at my short, fuzzy friend.

"We need to find a way to make Adam feel more like part of the family."

Right after we went for our walk.

CHAPTER 2

Garrett

PORTLAND WAS EDGING TOWARDS SUMMER. Which could mean anything, weather wise. Showers or sun. Cool or hot days. In other words, Portland in late spring and early summer was as unpredictable as a drunk drag queen with smeared lipstick in a karaoke bar. You never knew which way she was going to lurch, and what the outcome would be, but it was always entertaining.

Marsha and Klaus trotted happily ahead of John and me, their fuzzy little butts like white beacons leading us forward. It was a Sunday, and we were out running errands and enjoying getting some Vitamin D that didn't come in squishy gel-tablet form.

I didn't open my shop until noon on Sundays. I figured everyone around Pride Street wanted time to sleep in. That included John and me. Besides, I had cleverly designed my Sunday hours to catch the after-brunch crowds.

It being early June, the cherry trees had long since dropped their blossoms and the elms and maples were in full leaf, providing shade, which was good as today was one of the hot sunny ones.

Klaus and Marsha both paused to sniff something in front of the closed-until-lunch bar. Knowing what spilled out of the place at two in the morning, I really didn't want to know what they found so interesting.

Sunlight glistened on their fur and on a slick of what could be dried soda or who knows what at my feet. I took a step back.

"Are you working today?" I asked John. He shook his head.

"No. I finished the current draft and want to give it a day or two to percolate before I do one last pass and hand it off to my first reader."

He tugged on Klaus's leash, and we continued our walk.

"I was planning on doing some work in the garden, and if you're really nice to me, I'll cook you dinner."

"Oh?" I said. "Would you? I'll be soooo nice. As a matter of fact, I think you deserve some flowers."

Marsha began tugging again. I tugged back, which got me an annoyed look over her shoulder. I grinned at her little tri-color head. She really was a pretty dog.

"Well," John said, "we have plenty of flowers in the garden, along with salad greens, but I wouldn't say no to a small bouquet for my office."

He leaned over and gave me a peck on the cheek, which made me smile even wider. I really do love my man. By this time, we were approaching Bruiser's Best Beans, which meant controlling the corgis became a real effort. At least for me. John worked out for the both of us, I always said, but maybe my daily walks needed to be supplemented with a pushup or two.

Marsha was practically pulling my arm from its socket

and both dogs' tails wagged like flags semaphoring in a high wind.

I laughed. "Guess we're not stopping at Petunia's first. You might have to wait on those flowers. Maybe I'll stop and get some after work."

"Yeah," John said. "These two are not going to let us pass up Bruiser's."

Bruiser's Best Beans is run by our favorite lesbian couple, Bex and Jackie. They're both sweethearts and their English Bulldog, Bruiser, was one of Klaus and Marsha's best dog friends. As a matter of fact, all three of them had a little crush on each other. Sure enough, Bruiser came out to greet us, his broad white barrel chest almost the same width as his smashed in face. He was drooling and snorting and wiggling his tawny fur covered butt as hard as he could.

Marsha yipped in delight, and Klaus warbled out a happy greeting of his own.

"Okay, you two, simmer down," John said. "We're almost there."

We reached the tables out in front of the café which were packed as per usual on a beautiful Sunday. The dogs greeted each other, sniffing and barking and wagging.

I couldn't help but smile myself. It was a gorgeous day, and their joy was infectious.

"Why don't you go get our coffee and their t r e a t s," I said, spelling out the last word.

John arched an eyebrow at me. "You know they can spell, right?"

He was correct. At least for certain words.

After a quick peck on my cheek, John went inside and I looked around, hoping to find a table in the shade. An arguing couple got up, speaking in hushed tones. I got into position. One stalked off to the left, the other brushed past me and the dogs.

"Score!" I said to the trio at my feet. We all hurried over to the empty four-top picnic style table and parked ourselves, myself on a bench against the café wall and the three dogs at my feet.

They whuffed and snuffled at each other for a bit before settling down. It made me wonder what they talked about sometimes. John and I had considered getting those pet communication buttons, but always decided we really did not want to give Marsha any more power and authority in our household than she already had.

Maybe that was wrong of us, but you live with Marsha and see just how much more strong-willed communication you want to put up with.

Since it was warm out, there was a nice parade of people showing off. Big bears of men in loose jeans with tight t-shirts showing off their bellies and muscular arms, beards flowing down to touch the cotton. Women in skirts and shorts, laughing with each other over lattes or iced tea. A group of four coasted by on bicycles, out for a Sunday ride.

Two older men in linen pants and loose shirts held hands with a chubby toddler who walked in between them. Could be a grandchild, or an honorary niece or nephew. Because some of our own families still rejected us, our communities tended toward found or extended families that came in all different formations. I loved that about us. We turned disfunction and pain into a positive. Sure, it was by necessity, but that didn't mean it wasn't an effective strategy.

A cat walked by on a leash, which caused Klaus and Marsha to burst into barking. Bruiser? That dog is chill.

"Marsha! Klaus! Calm down!"

They both looked at me as if I was being completely unreasonable, but Bruiser backed me up with a lazy woof just as John returned with our lavender lattes, scones, and dog treats.

The first sip of sugary, caffeinated goodness hit my bloodstream, and I sighed in contentment, with John at my side.

Life was good on Pride Street. This was the world I enjoyed, the one I championed, and the one I hoped would never go away.

Ron from Bones, Dogs, and Harmony walked up with his old black lab Fred walking calmly along and his African gray parrot, Josephine Baker, cursing from his shoulder. Bones, Dogs, and Harmony is our local one-stop pet shop and vinyl record store. Ron had found a way to combine his two interests into a thriving business, and more power to him. Success couldn't have happened to a nicer guy.

He paused at our table, lowered his dark glasses, and smiled. Ron is a big, warm, friendly sort, with long dark locs flowing down his back and a collection of geeky T-shirts interspersed with old concert T-shirts. Today's shirt was the classic Run DMC logo.

Fred greeted the other dogs, and Josephine Baker squawked, "Hello, queer friends!"

We laughed.

"Did she just learn that?" I asked.

"Yeah. Yarrow spent hours teaching her. And I'm not sure if it's a good thing or not," Ron said.

"Please, join us," I said. "Fred can visit while you go inside."

"Thanks. I was wondering how I was going to get a

seat and had resigned myself to heading to the Park Blocks instead."

The Park Blocks were exactly what they sounded like, a narrow strip of grass and trees the width of one city block, but stretching over several, forming a strange, linked recreation space with sculptures, swing sets, and benches.

"Lucky for us that a couple finished their Sunday morning breakfast fight right when we showed up!" I quipped.

Ron left Fred, and he and Josephine Baker trundled into Bruiser's Best Beans.

"What a perfect day," John said. "I'll be glad to be out in the garden. Wish you could join me."

"I do too, but I've gotta make enough money to keep us in arugula."

Then the uproar began.

CHAPTER 3

Marsha

I LEAPT TO MY FEET, growling, swiveling my head to see what was wrong. All I could see were feet.

That's the trouble with being a corgi. Sure, I was well suited to pick things up from the ground, and my nose was at prime sniffing level, but sometimes? A dog wanted to see something besides chair legs, tree trunks, and shoes.

"Petunia! What's the matter?" Garrett leapt up and grabbed a sobbing person. She wore pink high-top sneakers and white jeans that were so short I could see a flash of pale skin between where the jeans ended and the shoes began.

Petunia. She ran Garrett and John's favorite flower shop. Flower Frenzy. It was the one they visited for special occasions, or as John sometimes said, "When Garrett needs to know I love him, just because."

I liked flowers well enough but preferred them in the ground. I didn't quite understand the appeal of cutting things just so they'd die and make the water green and stinky.

Both Klaus and I were on our feet, while Fred and

Bruiser remained lying down. At least they both lifted their heads.

"How can you stay so calm?" I asked them.

Bruiser snorted because that's what bulldogs do, and Fred woofed softly.

"We're older than you. We've learned to conserve our energy until we know we're needed. Besides, it's human drama. You know how they are."

I did know, but that didn't mean human drama didn't concern me. As a matter of fact, sometimes it concerned me a lot. I mean, what if a human couldn't give me treats anymore? What then?

Besides, I didn't like it when Garrett or John got upset. A dog can provide comfort to humans, and I think we should. Even though I have my own life to live, I don't want to go it alone.

Garrett and Ron finally got Petunia settled on one of the benches, with Ron and Josephine Baker at her side. I put my chin on her leg as she sobbed into Garrett's hand-kerchief. I could see she was smearing pink lipstick all over the cloth. Garrett was going to have a hard time getting that thing clean.

Petunia is a very colorful human. She is skinny, with a tiny pot belly, and has very pale skin that she tries to dress up with bright makeup in what John sometimes calls "loud colors." I don't understand how something you look at can be loud, but again, that's humans for you. I mean, what does hot pink lipstick have to do with "using my indoor voice"? How can both my voice and Petunia's lipstick be loud?

"Petunia, sweetie, you okay?" Ron was asking.

Petunia sniffed and stroked my head. I don't even think she realized she was doing it. See what I mean about dogs and comfort? Just being near a human is enough sometimes.

"Sapphire is missing."

"She ran away?" Garrett asked. "That doesn't seem like her."

Sapphire is a big, fluffy gray cat who lives with Petunia. She's a show cat, which makes her kind of snobby. Plus, she always reminds us of it. Every. Single. Time. We see her. Sometimes I get fed up and snap.

Oh. And she hates it when I say she's gray. "I'm silver!" she says, in her snottiest voice. I used to respond with "what's the difference" until I'd been swatted one to many times.

After a while, we made an agreement that Sapphire doesn't swipe at us, or lord it over us *too* much, and we don't bark or chase or bite her. Or call her gray. Luckily, we're not at the flower shop much, so it's a fairly easy agreement to uphold.

"She would never!" Petunia's lips trembled. Her skin looked funny. Wobbly. Like it was starting to slide off her chin. Usually, her face didn't look that way. Maybe when Petunia got upset, her skin began to melt. Or maybe that was more makeup. "Besides, we have a big show coming up, and she needs to prepare!"

Petunia began wailing. It sounded terrible.

"Klaus!" I woofed. *"Do you think Petunia's face is melting?"*

He tilted his little tan and white head and perked up his big ears.

"It does look a little funny. Probably because she's crying."

Huh. Okay.

Bex came out from inside the café, looking around to see where the disturbance was coming from, her short blonde hair shining in the sun. She wore jeans, a white singlet T-shirt covered by a black and burgundy striped vest, and big black boots I really wanted to bite.

Not that I wanted to bite Bex. Bex and Jacki were both really nice and gave us treats. But those boots? I bet they tasted like heaven.

She came over, a white dishrag in hand, face scrunched up with worry.

"Petunia? What happened?" She looked at the sobbing woman, then at Garrett, John, and Ron. I could see the question in her eyes.

"Sapphire is missing," Ron replied.

Fred woofed in agreement. *"Cat did a runner."*

I looked at Fred, startled. Everyone who knew Sapphire would know that cat would never run anywhere. She had it too good.

"Sapphire does not run," Klaus said.

I almost laughed. That was just how Sapphire would say it.

"Why else would she be missing?" Fred asked, his voice reasonable. *"I mean, she isn't very friendly, so it isn't like anyone would take her."*

Well, the old lab had a point in his glossy black head, I had to admit.

"You're all fools," Bruiser whuffed. *"Remember, Sapphire is one of those valuable cats."*

"Valuable cats?" Klaus tilted his head in confusion. I did, too.

"I mean, she's always saying that, but valuable how?" I asked. *"She doesn't even talk human like Josephine Baker."*

All Sapphire did was sit and preen.

"Who's a smart girl?" Josephine squawked.

I glared at the parrot, who ruffled her feathers, but settled back down on Ron's shoulder again.

"And she doesn't do tricks, like Fred used to. So, what makes her valuable? Her prissy attitude? The fact that she does those dumb shows she's always on about?" I really didn't get it.

Bruiser looked at me with his watery eyes. *"Some dogs and cats cost a lot of money. Even you and Klaus cost money. Not as much as Sapphire, though."*

"How about you and Fred?" Klaus asked.

"We both came from a shelter," Fred replied. *"We're only valuable because people love us."*

Bruiser farted loudly.

"Bruiser!" Bex admonished.

"Good thing we're outside," I heard Garrett say to John.

"She was stolen," Petunia wailed into the summer air. "Someone took my baby! And right before a competition!"

Some animals were worth stealing? For money? I mean, sure, Sapphire competed with other cats for most beautiful or snooty, or something, but I had no idea there was money involved.

A corgi can learn something new every day.

But sometimes? The things I learned weren't very nice.

CHAPTER 4

Garrett

I LEFT Ron and John to take care of Petunia and headed to my shop. Along with our classic Craftsman house, Dandy Decor & Design is my pride and joy. Slipping my key in the old-fashioned lock, I opened the door and rolled up the front door blind. The "open" sign would need to wait, though.

I did a quick walk-through, skimming through the Art Deco and mid-century modern sections before heading deeper in, toward the Victorian and Craftsman sections. I'm a lover of the latter two styles, but what can I say? Queer people seem to like deco and mid-mod. And the 1980s, a design era that personally gives me hives, but I stock a small collection of pieces, including the perennially popular Patrick Nagel posters, with their bold, graphic designs.

A couple of books had fallen over in the Craftsman section. I righted them on top of the sturdy sideboard and adjusted a vase, too. It was important to set things up to look as if they were grouped in someone's home. Other than designers and antique pickers, most people have trouble imagining how objects will work in their homes unless prodded by a clear visual.

This turned out well for me. I've been interested in design since I was a child in nowhere Oregon. That was the first thing that made me stand out to all the bullies. The second was the fact that I'm small. And the third? That it was clear way back then that I wasn't an actual girl. Kids can smell difference from a mile off, their noses keener than Klaus or Marsha's.

Add in a touch of neurodivergence? Let's just say I was pretty miserable until the theater geeks found me in high school and put me to work on props and building sets. Once I was old enough, I escaped to Portland to study design and become my best, queer, transgender self.

A knock came at the front door. I took a breath and settled a smile on my face. As a small business owner, being friendly and welcoming to clients was a must. As an introvert? Let's just say I've figured out strategies to make it work. Affirmations, meditation, and making myself take a breath and smile were all part of that.

And a well-chosen necktie and crisp white shirt never hurt.

Glancing at my watch, I saw that I was two minutes past official opening. The knock came again. Clearly, someone was impatiently waiting for the new shipment of mid-mod lamps.

"Coming!" I called out, and hurried my way back toward the front, sparing one longing glance at the burgundy curtain that sequestered the back rooms from the main area of the store. I hadn't had a chance to put the kettle on. At ten o'clock every morning, I switch from coffee to English Breakfast tea. And after noon? I switch to flavored water or herbal brews, depending on the season.

A person had their face pressed against the front glass of the door, which meant I'd be cleaning smudges off after they left. Why didn't people ever think of that?

As I got closer, skirting an overstuffed Art Deco armchair, I saw that it was Daniel, the owner of How We Roll, our favorite sushi restaurant. Daniel is a bit of a pill but had lightened up after I'd helped figure out who killed one of his waiters.

"Hello Daniel, what can I do for you this morning?"

I ushered him into the shop. Daniel was a handsome, Japanese American man, just a bit older than I am, with a slightly pockmarked face and silver threaded through his dark hair.

"Did you hear about Sapphire?"

Huh. That was unexpected.

I led him to the counter, where I fired up the cash point and glanced at my appointment book.

"I did. We ran into Petunia at Bruiser's this morning. She seems devastated."

But I was trying to figure out why Daniel cared. Even though we were all members of the LGBTQIA-BA—aka the Queer Business Association—he never exactly took much interest in the rest of us, preferring to do things his own way. I puttered about, waiting for his response.

He sniffed. I looked up, startled. Were those tears in his eyes? Or grass allergies?

"I don't think you know this, but…I have two Siamese cats. And I've been thinking about entering them into shows. They both qualify."

"I didn't know, Daniel." Because he never talked about them, never shared pictures on his phone while cooing, like other animal owners…and I'd also never run into him at Bones, Dogs, & Harmony picking up cat treats, either.

But knowing Daniel, he likely got treats shipped in from France, or something.

Did I mention he's a bit of a snob?

Daniel looked around the store, as if he wasn't the one who'd come in to talk to me. But it didn't seem like he'd be getting to the point any time soon.

"Daniel? Are you worried about your cats?"

He nodded, relief flooding his face. "I knew you of all people would understand! The way you and John dote on your corgis…" He looked around again. "Where are they?"

"They stayed with John." Okay. Time to be blunt. "But I still don't know why you're here."

His eyes grew fierce, and he leaned over the counter, pinning me with his eyes as if he was an owl and I was a mouse.

"You have to help me protect them."

I leaned back. "Me? Why me?"

"You…" He waved his hands in the air as if illustrating something. But I had no idea what that might be.

"I what?"

"You help people with things. Look at what you did for Saschi."

Well, Saschi was still dead, so I didn't see how what I did was very helpful after all. But we did find their killer, so I guess there's that. And the result was a tighter-knit community, so I supposed that was good, too.

"I still don't see, exactly, what you want me to do, Daniel. I mean, wouldn't you be better off going to Ron's shop or the vet and getting one of those GPS tags for their collars? Or a microchip?"

He shuddered, bringing a hand to his chest as if appalled.

"The princesses do not wear collars! They don't like them. And I feel bad at the thought of chipping them." He looked uncomfortable. "I know most owners of pure-bred animals get them chipped, but it just doesn't seem right to me."

I leveled my gaze at him. "Daniel. Get the cats some sparkly rhinestone collars. They'll love them." And if they didn't? Well, they'd get used to them. "And get GPS tags with their names on them. Ron sells both."

Daniel narrowed his eyes at me. We both knew that statement about Ron was a dig. Members of the Queer Business Association were supposed to support other small business owners, and the fact that he had cats and didn't shop at Ron's? We both knew I could cause a stink about it if I wanted to.

As threats go, it was a mild one, but come on!

Finally, Daniel nodded.

"Okay. Thank you. I will." He headed to the front door but turned before he opened it. "But I still expect you to come up with something. People can't just go around taking other people's friends!"

He stormed out the door, the chimes following him out into the street.

As I stared at his retreating back, I wondered what, exactly I was supposed to do about any of it. All of a sudden I wanted nothing more than to be in the back garden, digging in the flower beds with John and the dogs.

Instead, I had a business to run, and apparently a mystery to solve.

CHAPTER 5

Marsha

KLAUS and I decided we'd had enough of digging and were sprawled beneath a Japanese maple tree in the corner of the garden. Klaus's eyes were closed in corgi bliss as I cleaned my paws and watched John. He'd taken his shirt off, and the sun gleamed on his golden-brown skin. John could do that. If Garrett ever worked with his shirt off, he turned bright red, and John scolded him.

Some humans are designed for more sun than others, I guess. Kind of like dogs. Some dogs have fur too thick to handle the heat. My own black coat tended to make me a bit warm. John called me a "shade-seeking missile" sometimes. Whatever that meant. I mean, I do enjoy a nice patch of shade, which is why I love our neighborhood—so many trees!—but I wasn't sure what a missile was.

"Klaus?" I asked.

"Hmm?" His voice told me he was about to drift off to sleep.

"Can you wake up for a minute?" I barked a little louder.

He snorted and shook his head, looking around the garden, then at me. *"What's happening?"*

"Nothing," I said, watching John pull more weeds. We'd started off working in the raised beds, which didn't really have weeds, but he'd turned his attention to the low beds that snaked around the grass in the middle. There were lots of weeds there. John and Garrett hated weeds.

I thought they were kind of pretty.

"Then why do I have to wake up?"

"Because we need a plan to help Petunia and Sapphire," I replied, keeping my voice reasonable, even though I would have thought it was obvious. I'd learned the hard way that getting impatient with Klaus was useless.

"Why us?" he asked, chewing on some grass, which he would probably barf up later. Klaus has a delicate stomach. Like a cat.

"Because it's our job! We're the Pride Street Corgi Detectives!"

He sat up, head tilted in interest. *"We are?"*

I'd just made that up, but really liked the sound of it.

"Yes," I woofed. *"We are."*

"Wow! That sounds really important! I always wanted to be important!"

I drew myself up and barked. *"It's not about being important, Klaus, it's about solving things and helping people."*

"Oh," he said, deflating slightly.

I was lying. It was totally about being important. But Klaus didn't need to know that.

Klaus quickly perked up again. *"I guess that's a good thing though. Solving things and helping people."*

"What are you two talking about?" John called over.

"Should we tell him?" Klaus woofed.

I looked at our human, who wiped his brow with the back of his hand.

"Not yet. But maybe he'll take us on another walk."

We both trotted over to John just as the back gate rattled.

"Intruder! Intruder!" I barked, then started growling.

"Marsha P, shh!" John admonished, then stood up, wiping his face with his white T-shirt before putting it back on.

Klaus and I ran toward the gate just as Princess Sparkle Toes tripped back.

"Yooo hoo!" she called, waving one white hand.

I squinted.

Princess Sparkle Toes was very, very bright. It was like staring at the sun. She wore a summer yellow frock that swung around her calves, and some weird shoes with yellow cloth straps that wound up her legs and made her teeter on her toes.

John wears shoes like that sometimes, but I notice they stay home when he goes running.

"Princess!" Klaus barked, his tail wagging happily.

"Hello my precious doggies! And you, too, you handsome man."

PST turned toward John with a smile on her orange-painted lips.

There was movement in the second story bedroom. Adam stared out the window. I barked up at him, and he waved.

I wished there was a way to get him out of the house. I think he would enjoy the garden as much as Klaus and I do. We also needed to work on getting him reunited with the little dog he'd mentioned once upon a time.

"John, I must speak with you and Garrett! Where is he?"

John bent and began to gather his tools, then crossed

the lawn and turned off the hose at the source. Drat. That meant no play time in the water after he was done.

"He's at the store, working. Can it wait?"

"Oh no, no, no, it cannot!" PST pursed her orange lips, fingers stroking the bright gold medal she always wore. It was a star shape, but not like some of the ones the Wiccans in the neighborhood wore. Theirs had five points. Her star had six.

"You must take me to him, post haste!"

John smiled. "You do know you sound like someone in an old melodrama, don't you?"

PST sniffed. "Well, this *is* Pride Street! It is filled with melodrama. Now—" She waved her hand in a circle, then pointed to the house. "Get your cute runner's butt inside, get cleaned up, and take me to your husband!"

"Sparkle Toes, before I interrupt Garrett at work, is there something I can do to help, first?"

I sniffed around her yellow shoes and heard her sob.

Looking up, I saw her face crumple. I licked her shin in sympathy, and she jumped and shrieked.

"Oh! Marsha P. Johnson. You scared me."

John made a clicking noise and crouched down. I trotted toward him, the grass soft on my paws. Neither human seemed mad, which was good, because I only had the best intentions.

This time, at least.

John scratched my head. Klaus nosed in on the action.

"Tell me what's wrong," John said.

"It's my hamster, Mr. Cheeks."

We all looked at Princess Sparkle Toes. She had a hand to her mouth, as if trying to hold something back. Finally, the dam burst.

"He's disappeared!" she wailed. "At first, I thought he

must be in my apartment somewhere. But then I heard about Sapphire, and…"

She broke down.

John gave her a quick hug and a pat on the back. She sniffed, then blew her nose.

"We'll help you," he said, then turned to us and clapped his hands. "Come on, you two! Let's get those paws cleaned off. Then let's go for a walk."

He held the door for Princess Sparkle Toes, who walked across the back porch like she was human royalty.

I matched her stride, holding my nose in the air.

I heard Klaus laughing at me from behind, but what did I care? I was head of a detective agency now and needed to act the part.

There were hamsters to find. And cats.

And I was just the corgi to do it.

CHAPTER 6

Garrett

PRINCESS SPARKLE TOES' apartment is five blocks off Pride Street, heading north, away from downtown. It's shaded by maples and elms. Unlike the east side of the river, most of the trees over this way are a mixture of cherry, ginkgo, maple, and elm. Across the river, you get a lot more Douglas fir and spruce, making the neighbor-hoods feel wilder than they do over our way.

John and I walked next to Sparkle Toes, with Klaus and Marsha leading our strange parade. Sparkle Toes walked as if dejected, and I didn't blame her. I might personally find hamsters a bit ridiculous, but a companion animal is a companion animal, and to have one missing? That had to be wrenching.

I don't know what I'd do if Marsha and Klaus were stolen from us. Though the scamps escaped on occasion, they always came back soon enough.

Even Marsha—the usual instigator—knows where her food and favorite nap spot is.

Sparkle Toes paused in front of a three-story blue and pink Victorian to fish keys from the yellow purse that matched the rest of her ensemble. It was a building I always admired, with intact gingerbread at the peak and around the porch, and fish scale siding on the top floor. Amazingly, it had been designed as four apartments, rather than being an old grande dame chopped up by a landlord.

Sparkle Toes, of course, lived in the very top flat, under the eaves. We entered a small, wood-paneled foyer, and Sparkle Toes started the climb.

Klaus looked up the uncarpeted stairs and whined. Marsha just looked from me to John, as if to say, *what exactly are you going to do about this situation?*

I sighed and hefted her into my arms. John did the same with Klaus.

"You two are so spoiled!" I said, starting the long climb.

Marsha barked in protest. I laughed and followed the splash of yellow up the stairs, reminded once again that I need to do more than take the dogs for walks.

Princess Sparkle Toes kept up a running commentary, not even pausing for breath between floors. And she was walking in espadrilles, while I had on sensible leather brogues. But then, she did this climb several times a day and wasn't carrying twenty-five pounds of corgi in her arms.

"I've got to start working out," I groaned.

"Any time you want, babe." John's voice was mild, but I could hear his amusement.

"I just hope Mr. Cheeks is okay!" Princess Sparkle Toes was saying. She'd repeated the same thing at least thirty times in the past five minutes, so I'd kind of tuned her out.

By the time we reached Princess Sparkle Toes' flat, I was sweating under my shirt collar and had dog hair stuck to the damp skin on my neck. I plopped Marsha down on the small landing with a sigh of relief and glared at my husband, who wasn't even winded, let alone sweaty.

He shrugged and smiled. I wiped my face with my handkerchief and stuck out my tongue.

Sparkle Toes ushered us inside, leading us down a narrow hallway with white painted wainscoting. Sparkle Toes had hung bright splashes of art along the walls above the traditional dado rail. We passed a small bathroom on the left, and a bedroom on the right.

Then we stepped into the main living space and I gasped.

The place was a marvel of a Victorian apartment. Tall, peaked ceilings with cunning bookcases built into the knee walls led to a huge arched window that took up most of the front wall, with a view of the trees outside. A purple loveseat was paired with two chairs upholstered in cream damask. No curtains blocked the view, and weren't needed, not with the way the trees and the building height sheltered the apartment from prying eyes.

A tidy kitchenette was behind us, clearly sharing a wall with the bedroom behind.

"Someone did an amazing job with this place," I said.

Sparkle Toes looked pleased. "I love it."

John and I took the dogs off leash, and they both began sniffing around, tails wagging with excitement.

We all followed their trajectory around the space. Though Sparkle Toes' eyes tracked Klaus and Marsha, it didn't seem as if she really saw them.

"Do you have anything that smells like Mr. Cheeks?" John asked.

Sparkle Toes startled, looking around as if she didn't know who had spoken.

She must really love Mr. Cheeks, to be so completely distracted. Either that, or something else was going on. As for me? I tried to keep my mind on the missing hamster, when really, I was itching to examine some of the antiques dotted around the living room space.

"I do. I have his favorite binkie."

She hurried to the bedroom in those marvelously ridiculous espadrille shoes.

Klaus woofed near a gorgeous wood sideboard, and Marsha trotted over.

"Find something?" I asked.

Klaus pawed the wood floors at the edge of the large patterned carpet that covered the bulk of the living room area, nicely separating it from the kitchen.

John and I looked at each other and walked closer as Marsha barked encouragement at Klaus.

"Did you find Mr. Cheeks?" I asked, crouching down. Would it really be this easy? Mr. Cheeks was just hiding?

Klaus continued pawing. I heard when one of his claws caught. There was a dragging sound across wood, and then Klaus yipped, snapped his jaws, and began running around the room, chased by Marsha who had started barking in earnest.

"What is happening?" Princess Sparkle Toes sounded breathless. She stood in the center of the little kitchen area, clutching a scrap of flannel. "Did they find Mr. Cheeks?"

"They found something," I said, darting after Klaus, as John and I did the catch-the-dogs dance. Both of us had our arms out, but as soon as one of us got close, Klaus dodged again, abetted by Marsha, who seemed to be doing her best to get in our way.

I collided with her furry butt and stumbled, barely

catching myself on the loveseat before I cracked my knees on the floor.

"Klaus Nomi!" John shouted. "Stop that. Put that down!"

He grabbed Klaus's scruff mid-run. Klaus's little paws scrabbled for purchase, and he whined.

"Drop it!" John said.

Klaus rolled his eyes back at my partner. I stifled a laugh. If you've never experienced corgi side-eye, just know that if it ever happens? The corgi is not impressed with whatever you're doing. As a matter of fact, if a corgi could spit, Klaus probably would.

John just held Klaus and stared back.

Marsha yipped.

Finally, Klaus dropped whatever was in his mouth, and John grabbed it, releasing the dog.

"What is it?" I asked.

Princess Sparkle Toes moved closer. We all peered down at what was in John's hand. Something glinted in his palm.

He held the small object to the light coming from the big arched window.

It was a dangling bauble. A crystal, like the kind that hung from a chandelier.

I glanced up. No chandelier in here.

"It's an earring," John said, holding it out toward Princess Sparkle Toes. "One of yours?"

She gasped and backed away, shaking her head.

Guess that was a no, then.

"Whose is it?" I asked. I plopped on the loveseat and was stroking Marsha's head. Klaus was still glued to John's ankles, looking up at his prize.

Sparkle Toes just kept shaking her head.

"I…I don't know." She worked the scrap of cloth—Mr. Cheeks' blanket—between her hands. If she wasn't careful, she'd rip the thing.

John looked at me, his handsome brow furrowed. I shrugged. It was clear that Sparkle Toes recognized the earring, so why wouldn't she say so?

Marsha left my side and walked calmly over to Sparkle Toes. Finally, she sat at her heels and barked.

"What does she want?"

"To sniff Mr. Cheeks' blanket," I said.

Sparkle Toes bent, holding out the flannel. Marsha sniffed at it delicately, then lunged, ripping the blanket out of Sparkle Toes' hands. Sparkle Toes shrieked and teetered on her yellow shoes.

"Marsha P.!" I leapt up and began to chase her, which she thought was great fun. She raced in a circle around the room, then zoomed down the short hallway. I heard scrabbling from the bedroom and followed.

I stopped in the doorway. Marsha was stock still in front of the gleaming old dresser, looking up at the empty hamster cage. She turned to me, eyes sorrowful, and whined. Then she dropped the little blanket.

"What's the matter, girl?" I asked softly.

Sparkle Toes crowded behind me. "What's happening? What has she found?"

Marsha turned from the dresser, squeezed past my legs, and headed toward the apartment door.

"I don't understand!" Princess Sparkle Toes wailed. "What did she find? What's happening?"

Marsha pawed at the front door. Klaus barked from the living room, then raced down the hall, almost colliding with Marsha's butt.

Both dogs looked back at us, clearly ready to go.

I looked past Sparkle Toes' shoulder. John put a finger to his lips and gave a slight shake of his head. Okay. Now I was confused.

"I'm sorry, Sparkle Toes," I said. "I really thought the dogs could help. But they're insisting on going."

"But...but... what about Mr. Cheeks?"

I reached out and gave her arm a squeeze. "We'll find him."

She sniffed.

"Promise?"

"Promise."

But deep in my heart, I knew that was as much of a lie as the one Princess Sparkle Toes had told us. She knew exactly whose earring Klaus had found.

And I had no idea how to find Mr. Cheeks.

Or whether the hamster was even still alive.

CHAPTER 7

Adam

THE HOUSE WAS BEAUTIFUL. Garrett really was a talented man. The old wood window casings, lintels, and floors were the same, but everything gleamed with the polish of restoration now. And the green fireplace tiles had been cleaned. When I was alive, they were soot stained and frankly, lighting the fireplace was a good way to die.

Garrett not only knew what he was doing, but the two men had more money than our ragtag bunch of gay activists and party boys.

The dogs made me miss my Lucy, though. I hoped she was someplace nice, and not pining after me.

There were footsteps on the front porch, then the sound of keys in the lock. Klaus and Marsha rushed in, barking wildly, heading my way. I smiled. How could I not. They were the cutest, those two. Almost as cute as the two men who followed them, pausing in the narrow foyer to remove their shoes.

I looked down at my own leather boots. I was no longer able to track a damn thing into the house, considering I couldn't even seem to leave the four walls. Marsha

P. Johnson was convinced I could make it to the front porch, and maybe even the back garden, but I hadn't risked it yet.

Maybe someday.

"So, are you going to tell me what you and Klaus are up to?" Garrett asked.

"Princess Sparkle Toes was lying," John replied. Both men headed to the kitchen, and John began to pull things from the refrigerator. Must be dinnertime.

Garrett leaned against one of the bright white counters —another change from when I was alive—and crossed his arms over his narrow chest.

"Even I could tell she was lying. But clearly you think you know something I don't."

John pulled out a saucepan and poured a stream of oil in, clicking the burner onto low. Garrett started scrubbing some vegetables as John chopped an onion.

I didn't miss chopping onions, that was for sure. But I did miss eating them. I missed eating, period. I missed a lot of things.

"The earring! She knew who the earring belonged to!" Klaus barked.

I looked down at the little tan and white corgi. ::*What are you talking about?*::

Marsha walked over. *"Klaus dug an earring out from behind Princess Sparkle Toes' couch."*

"We were looking for her hamster!" Klaus woofed.

Okay. This conversation was getting odd. But I'd grown to expect that when talking with these two. It was a funny thing, waking up in the back of my old closet and discovering that the only two people I could talk to were short and furry.

And not the kind of short and furry I used to like to date.

::Slow down. What happened to her hamster? And what's this about an earring?::

With a hiss and pop, John slid the chopped onion into the hot oil. I could almost smell it.

"Do you think the person with the earring stole Sapphire and Mr. Cheeks then?" Garrett was asking.

Sapphire and Mr. Cheeks? Sounded like a drag queen and last year's winner of Portland Mr. Leather.

John stirred the onions.

"I don't know, but something about this whole situation seems suspect. I mean, I get someone stealing Sapphire. She's a show cat, after all."

Oh. A cat. That made more sense.

"But a hamster?" John continued. "Why would anyone steal a hamster?"

I burst out laughing.

"Did you hear something?" Garrett asked, looking around the kitchen.

"Like what?" John asked.

Garrett shook his head but gave Klaus and Marsha a look. They were both still at my side, with Klaus's head nestled next to my boots. The two corgis had grown less shy about touching me, though they still winced a bit when I scratched their heads. Marsha says my fingers are really cold.

John added some pre-sliced chicken to the pan with the onions. Meanwhile, Garrett was staring at the doorway just behind my head. He stepped forward.

"Adam? Is that you?"

Marsha barked.

"Yes! Yes! Adam is right here!"

Klaus turned in a tight circle, tongue lolling. I laughed again. How could I help myself?

John paused his stirring and looked over. "The ghost is here?"

"I think so."

"Ask him if he knows anything about stolen pets."

::I don't know a thing about stolen pets. But if you two ever figure out how to get my dog Lucy to visit, I'd greatly appreciate it.::

Garrett gave the space over my shoulder one last look, then turned back to John.

"I want to dig through that box of his stuff again. See if there's anything that might help us connect to him."

"You mean, like the way psychics use psychometry? Getting information from objects people have touched," John said. "Huh. I have no idea whether that will work, but it seems worth a try. I bet he's lonely."

I stood very still. What a thought. That something of mine might allow John or Garrett to actually communicate with me? That would be… something.

Garrett got a bottle of white wine from the fridge and set about pouring two glasses. These two really were a lot more refined than my friends and I ever were. But then, they aren't dying off left and right, so probably don't feel the urge to cram as much partying, love, and anger into every day as we did.

"So, what do you think is happening?" Garrett asked John. The two clinked glasses.

"To your health," John said.

"Slainte," Garrett replied.

John turned heat down again, and both men stood and sipped their wine in silence for a moment.

"I think we need to figure out what Sparkle Toes is so

afraid of. And Marsha knows something, too. Did you see her response to Mr. Cheeks' cage?"

::*Marsha?*:: I asked the little tri-colored corgi.

"I think Mr. Cheeks died in his cage. At least, that's what it smelled like. Or something was rotting."

Wait a minute.

::*If Mr. Cheeks is dead, then why did this Princess Sparkle Toes say he was missing?*::

"That's what we're going to find out!"

The men kept talking, oblivious to our conversation, other than occasionally telling Marsha to quiet down.

::*Can I make you two a deal?*:: I asked.

"What?" Klaus barked.

::*If you help me find my dog, maybe I can help you find out whose earring it is.*::

Both dogs cocked their heads at me, looking confused.

"How is that going to happen?" Klaus asked. *"You don't even leave the house."*

::*You're going to tell me everything you find, aren't you? And bring me what you can, just like you did when your waiter friend was killed.*::

Marsha walked over and nudged my boots with her head. She passed halfway through the leather, but I didn't mind. I appreciated the gesture of comfort, all the same.

"We'll help you find your dog, Adam," she said. *"But even if we can't, you're one of our humans now."*

This time, instead of laughing, I felt like I was going to cry.

CHAPTER 8

Garrett

DINNER WAS DELICIOUS. It always was when John cooked.

"I'm exhausted," I groaned as I loaded the final plate into the dishwasher.

John stepped over and rubbed my shoulders. "You've had quite the day. We all have."

The dogs' eyes were drooping. I was drooping, too. I wanted nothing more than to take off my clothes, hop in the shower, then snuggle up in bed.

My phone buzzed in my pocket. I groaned again. Louder this time.

"Can I ignore that?" I asked.

John smiled at me. "You know you're too nosy for that."

I gave him a playful punch on the arm and fished my phone from my trouser pocket.

Come to Enrico's. There's someone here you have to see.

"No. No. No. No."

"What is it?"

I showed John my phone. "It's Daniel. He's being all dramatic."

"I really don't want to go out tonight. I've got a podcast interview tomorrow, and I need to talk to my editor."

We can't. I texted back. *Need to get up early.*

I'm coming over.

"What?" I practically shrieked. Marsha barked in alarm. "John! He says he's coming over!"

John just sighed. "I'll put on a pot of coffee. If Daniel says he's coming over, nothing we do or say will stop him. Let's just hope he's not bringing anyone else."

I scrubbed my hands over my face and shuffled into the living room to flop on the sofa. I was truly exhausted. The dogs clicked in and headed to the big dog bed near the cold fireplace, and John joined me.

It felt like we'd only been sitting for five minutes when there was pounding on our door.

My head flopped to the back of the couch, and I groaned again. Marsha stood, but Klaus didn't even raise his head. Poor thing must be tuckered out.

John rose—bless him—and answered the door.

"You are two old men!" Daniel's voice complained. I heard the thunk of his shoes dropping to the floor, followed by two lighter thunks, and then two more. Who else was here?

Had Daniel brought the whole nightclub back?

"I really don't see why you couldn't come out. It isn't as if you can't just walk to Enrico's from here!"

I turned. Daniel was followed by Petunia and Yarrow. All three of them looked upset.

"Coffee?" John asked.

"Yes, please," Petunia sniffed. She and Daniel took the

two chairs flanking the fireplace. Yarrow looked at the couch as if trying to decide where to sit.

Before I could offer them a chair, another knock came. This time, both dogs leapt up and started barking, but it was their happy barks, not their intruder barks.

Guess I had to answer it.

I shuffled to the big wood door, Klaus and Marsha at my stockinged feet, and opened it to Ron and Fred, whose tail wagged happily. Luckily Josephine Baker stayed in her cage at night, so I wouldn't have to put up with her comments.

"Come in," I said. "Join the party."

"You're having a party?" Ron asked as he toed his sneakers off. John has all our friends well trained, and I have to admit, the no-shoes rule keeps the house much cleaner.

"May as well be," I muttered.

John poked his head out of the kitchen.

"Hi Ron! Coffee?"

Ron's face lit up. "That'd be great!"

Pretty soon, we were all gathered around the coffee table, with the dogs happily crunching treats, half on and half off the big bed on account of Fred not quite fitting.

John sat next to me in the middle of the couch and poured out coffee and sparkling water, while Ron took up the other end. Yarrow grabbed a cushion from the couch and sank down bonelessly to the floor.

I turned to Daniel. His black, silver-shot hair looked mussed, and his eyes were slightly red. Petunia still sniffed into a voluminous handkerchief.

"Why are you all here?" I asked Daniel, then looked past John to Ron. "You too, Ron."

Ron gestured to Daniel. "You were here first."

"You'll never guess who was at Enrico's!"

"Not if you don't tell us," John replied, his voice dry.

"Your ex!" Petunia burst out. "That bitch was there, canoodling with Sweetheart Digs!"

Canoodling? Who even says that?

"And?" I asked. I was way too tired to be dealing with my heartbreaking ex, Vyviane, and the self-proclaimed Mayor of Pride Street, Sweetheart Digs. Vyviane was newly back in town and had briefly made the suspect list in the murder of Saschi, one of the waiters from Daniel's sushi restaurant.

If she was hanging out with Sweetheart Digs, she was up to something, but then, Vyviane always was. She's a shark, that woman. A gold-digging, opportunist shark. Which is why I didn't understand her interest in me. I must have just been a way to pass the time between marks.

"Do you think they have something to do with Sapphire's disappearance?" John asked Petunia.

Though what Vyviane would want with a pampered show cat, I wasn't sure. I mean, sure they're worth money, but they're also pretty high maintenance. Sweetheart Digs, though? I never knew what angle he might be running.

"That Vyviane is such a nasty piece of work!" Petunia burst out again. "We were sitting, having cocktails, minding our own business, when she waltzed right over and asked me how my cat was!"

Okay. This really was odd. Vyviane never cared one whit about anyone's lives, let alone their animals. The only time she cared was if she thought you could do something for her.

I sat up straight, suddenly awake.

"Wait a minute," I asked Petunia. "Do you have money?"

Petunia looked shocked, and then confused.

"Told you," Yarrow murmured.

Petunia looked from Yarrow to me, pink painted lips opening and closing like some strange, tropical fish.

"Wh-why would you ask me that?"

"Petunia, darling," Daniel said, leaning toward her, his coffee cup cradled in his hands. "Because money is the only thing Vyviane likes in this world."

"Told you she's only nice to rich people," Yarrow said, tugging at the hems of their burgundy trousers.

Petunia fanned her face with one hand.

"Petunia?" I asked. "Is there something you need to tell us?"

She really looked stricken.

"You may as well tell us, Petunia," Daniel said. "I mean, you did ask for our help."

"My great aunt died. Turned out she was a secret lesbian."

"I love a secret lesbian!" John gasped. I patted his thigh.

Petunia nodded. "I don't know how I never knew. She was ninety-five, though, so not exactly in her prime dating years when I was old enough to understand such things."

"And?" I asked.

Petunia turned her mascara ringed eyes my way. "She left me all her money. And there was a considerable amount."

My tired brain finally kicked in.

"Wait. Do you think Vyviane stole Sapphire? And what about Mr. Cheeks?"

"Mr. Cheeks?" Ron looked confused. "Sparkle Toes' hamster? Is he missing?"

"*I think he's dead!*" Marsha barked suddenly. It looked as if she was actually attending to the conversation. I sometimes wished I understood what she was saying.

But then I remembered she probably just wanted a snack. Corgis always want a snack.

"Sssh, girl. You already ate." Marsha looked at me as if I'd terribly betrayed her. Or as if I was dense. I turned back to Ron.

"Princess Sparkle Toes was in a tizzy, and Mr. Cheeks was not in his cage. But she didn't really give us any information on how he disappeared."

Which was strange, now that I thought of it. We'd gotten so caught up in the earring discovery, and then Marsha had acted weird and wanted to go.

I looked John.

"We never asked her how anyone would have gotten to Mr. Cheeks. Does he ever leave the apartment? I mean, I didn't even know she had a hamster."

John looked at Ron, who shrugged. "She brings him to the store sometimes. She has this little hamster carrying purse. It's pink."

Of course, she did. Then another thought occurred to me.

"Petunia? Daniel? What kind of earrings was Vyviane wearing?"

CHAPTER 9
Marsha

"WALK FASTER, KLAUS!"

I play-snapped at Klaus's heels and he growled. I was ready to growl myself. I was desperate to get to Bruisers for cookies and gossip. It was Garrett's day off from the shop, so he was wrangling both of us while John did some interview thing. John walked faster, but Garrett was easier to control by the sheer force of our bodies.

"I don't want to pull Garrett's arms out of their sockets! You know how he feels about that!"

Ewww. Gross.

"He doesn't mean that literally, fuzz head."

"You're a fuzz head, too!" Klaus barked.

"What are you two talking about? And why are you in such a hurry? I told you we'll see all your friends. First Bruiser's, then Ron's. But I want time to sit and read at Bruiser's and Ron doesn't open for a while, so cool your jets. Okay?"

"We don't have jets," Klaus woofed. *"But they might be fun."*

"If you weren't so lazy, you wouldn't need jets."

This time, Klaus snapped at me.

But it was true, I didn't need jets. I was plenty fast when Garrett and John would let us off leash. Maybe Garrett would take us to the park today. I could use a good run.

After I gathered some clues.

I tugged harder, and Garrett said a bad word. But seriously, couldn't he see how important it was to talk to people? I wasn't even pausing to sniff, which, now that I thought of it, I should be. I mean, maybe I'd smell Sapphire somewhere.

Slowing down, I sniffed some bushes and a fence post. Just dogs. No cat scent anywhere.

"First you're in a rush, and now you want to check messages?" Garrett said.

I didn't pay any attention, just kept my nose to the ground. I mean, not literally, but I was sniffing all the same.

Finally, we turned the corner, and Bruiser gave a joyful bark, wagging his butt with all his might. He could've run up to meet us, but Bruiser is lazier than Klaus. If I had that much trouble breathing, I probably would be, too. Not everyone can have long, elegant noses and superior lung capacity.

"Bruiser!" Klaus said.

"Did you find anything out?" I barked.

"I did! I did!" Bruiser practically hopped in excitement, which was a sight to see. His white and tan barrel of a body levitated three inches off the sidewalk.

"Tell us!" Klaus yapped.

Garrett sighed. "You three. I'm glad you like each other, but you act like you've been apart for weeks! You just saw each other yesterday."

He tied us to one of the rings outside, near a table shaded by a big elm tree. Once Garrett headed inside, we both turned back to Bruiser.

A string of drool dangled from the side of his mouth.

"Marsha?" Bruiser asked. He looked confused. Uh oh. Had he started talking while I was mesmerized by the disgusting wad of saliva descending to the sidewalk?

"Sorry! I was thinking. What did you say?"

"I said that terrible, skinny blonde woman was in earlier. Jacki and Bex don't like her."

"Vyviane?" I asked. *"I hope she's gone!"* If she wasn't, our visit with Bruiser would be cut short. No way was Garrett going to be able to relax and read if she was around.

Bruiser shook his head. "She was only here for a minute. Jacki complained that she didn't even order coffee."

Two men headed toward us. One of them pushed a baby stroller. The toddler inside waved its arms and shrieked. I winced.

"Dog! Dog! Dog!"

The toddler pumped its chubby little arms.

"Yes, those are dogs! Smart girl, Annabelle! Would you like to see if they want pets?"

No way. Little Annabelle would pull my ears with her spit-covered hands. It had happened before. I slowly backed away, but Klaus, the doofus, stood up and stuck his nose right in the stroller!

The toddler shrieked again. Bruiser looked at me, eyes pained.

Klaus gave a sharp yip. Sure enough, one of Annabelle's little hands was wrapped around his ear, and she was pulling him toward her mouth.

"No, Annabelle! Be nice to the doggy! Gentle!" said one dad, while the other tried to pry her fist from Klaus's ear.

Annabelle screamed. Klaus dug in and tried to pull away, claws grabbing for purchase on the sidewalk.

"Pull, Klaus!"

He whined. Okay. Enough of this.

I lunged toward the stroller, barking. Annabelle started sobbing and screaming. Great.

But at least she dropped Klaus's ear.

"Marsha P. Johnson!" Garrett hurried over, iced coffee drink sloshing over the rim of his big glass. "What in the world are you doing?"

"Your dog attacked our daughter!" one of the men said.

I growled. *"Not true! She attacked Klaus!"*

Klaus whined some more. Bruiser licked his ear.

Annabelle kept screaming.

"I'm so sorry," Garrett said. "She's usually so good. Did something happen?"

"Well..." said the other man as his partner said, "Nothing."

"Come on, honey. Annabelle grabbed the other dog's ear and wouldn't let go. I think Marsha here was just trying to help her friend, weren't you girl?"

Garrett sagged with relief.

"Well. Again. I'm sorry."

The one man set his mouth, but his partner patted his arm. "Let's just go, honey. I think Annabelle could use an early nap."

The two men continued on their way.

"You two," Garrett said, shaking his head. "I was only in there for a few minutes."

He set his coffee down and crouched, holding out a hand toward Klaus. "You okay there, buddy?"

Klaus nuzzled his hand and got a scratch on the head in return. No scratches for Marsha P. Johnson, though, and I was the one who saved Klaus in the first place.

Hmph.

Finally, we were all settled again, fresh bowls of water nearby, and a cookie for each of us. Garrett opened his book and sipped his coffee.

"What did Vyviane want?" I asked Bruiser.

"She wanted to know if she'd dropped an earring here."

Klaus looked at me. I looked at Klaus.

"What?" Bruiser asked.

"Klaus found an earring at Princess Sparkle Toes' apartment. And her hamster is missing."

"Or dead!" Klaus woofed.

Right. *"Or dead."*

CHAPTER 10

Garrett

LUCKILY, no more toddlers happened by, which meant I had an uninterrupted hour of reading in the shade as the dogs visited. They had a lot to talk about, which was strange. Usually, they just slept in a heap.

I glanced at my watch. Ron's was open. Time to check that errand off my list.

"Okay, kids, I'm going to run my glass inside. Say goodbye to Bruiser!"

I dropped my empty pint glass in the tub near the counter. Bex waved me over.

"Hey, we were too busy when you got your coffee, and I didn't want to say this in front of other people, but did you know Vyviane is still around?"

"I've heard. I mean, she was around for Saschi's memorial a couple of months ago, but since I hadn't seen her, I was hoping she'd headed back out of town."

Vyviane was like a butterfly, flitting from place to place, but instead of pollen or nectar, she was seeking money. And if she couldn't have money? Well, she might take on a plaything to pass the time for a while.

That was me, once upon a time. The plaything, I mean, not the butterfly.

Bex frowned. "Well, seems like she's back to stay. At least for now. Still a major jerk. Came in. Asked questions. Didn't order a thing."

Typical Vyviane. If no one else was buying, she was a cheapskate. All she had to do was sell off a couple of her purses, and she'd be set for ready cash. The one time I had suggested it, I'd almost lost my head. That was the beginning of the end. After that? She'd started being cruel.

"What did she want?" I sighed.

"Well, she asked about you, but we deflected." Bex jerked her head to her partner Jacki, who snorted and went back to restocking the fridge behind the counter. "She also wanted to know if we'd found an earring."

I stilled. "An earring?"

"Yeah. You know anything about that?"

I scanned the coffee shop, buying a few seconds' time. "I may have. But I don't want to spread rumors, you know?"

Bex tilted her head back and laughed, then ran a hand through the short, bleached blonde mop that crowned her narrow head.

"You know Pride Street runs on rumors, Garrett. And I also know you don't spread gossip for gossip's sake."

She gave me an expectant look. I just frowned.

"Your call," she said. "But if you need to talk about it, we're here."

"Thanks."

I gathered up Klaus and Marsha and we headed down the street to Bones, Dogs, and Harmony, the corgi's second favorite place. After Bruiser's, of course.

I pushed open the door, greeted by the sound of classic

soul. Ron must be pensive, because it was not the upbeat, Motown version. This was some serious Marvin Gaye material. People wandered the pet supply aisles, and a couple of others rifled through records on the Harmony side of the shop.

I let the doggos off leash. They ran to greet Fred, Ron's black lab.

"Hello Handsome!" the gray parrot squawked.

"Hello to you, too, Josephine Baker," I replied.

"Who's a pretty girl?" she asked, dancing sideways on her perch in the front window.

"You are!" I said.

Ron laughed from behind the counter. "Doesn't she know it? How you doing today, man? Any news since last night?"

I leaned against the counter.

"I was hoping you would have some. Bex and Jacki say Vyviane came by, looking for a missing earring."

Ron wound his fingers around a loc, twisting the hairs near the base of his skull. He only did that in public when he was nervous. Or thinking. He must have realized he was doing it, because he dropped his hand and leaned across the counter, lowering his voice.

"You think Vyviane and Sparkle Toes…?"

"I don't know what to think. Why in the world would Sparkle Toes be helping Vyviane?"

But Sparkle Toes really hadn't wanted to talk about that earring. So maybe they were up to something.

"And what about Sweetheart Digs?" I asked. "He was with her at Enrico's last night. And wait a minute… we got sidetracked last night! You came over to tell us something!"

Ron shuffled back, looking uncomfortable. He looked around the store. I did, too. Everyone seemed occupied.

"Danger!" Josephine Baker squawked.

Uh oh. What did the parrot know that I didn't?

"Hush, Josephine," Ron sighed. "She's been agitated all morning."

He looked at the front window displays, but I could tell he wasn't seeing them or bird enclosures, chew toys, or other animal related objects.

I stared too. Roderick Gauge, another pasty, glasses wearing man like me—except he dresses more casually and he's not trans—peered into the window, his dark glasses shining in the sun. He gave a little wave, and I waved back.

"Last night, I was out walking Fred," Ron finally said. "He's an old man now, and needs a second walk to make sure he doesn't need to go out in the middle of the night."

I nodded encouragement, then gave a quick glance toward the back to make sure Marsha and Klaus weren't getting into mischief. Amazingly, they both contentedly chewed new toys I'd have to pay for while visiting with Fred.

Marsha's ears perked up, and she trained her dark brown eyes my way. I smiled, and she went back to chewing what looked like a rubber shoe.

"At any rate," Ron continued, "I saw something. Or I think I did. Could've been nothing."

"What was it?"

But right then, one of the vinyl lovers approached with a stack of discs.

Ron flipped through them, making appreciative comments at the selections of old soul, hip hop, and 1980s punk. Bad Brains was the final album. Too loud for me, but then, I'm more of a dance techno, big band, or classical kind of guy.

"Eclectic taste," I said.

The young woman smiled at me. She wore her tightly curled hair in a classic 80s fade. Everything old is new again. "My parents love this stuff. Grandparents, too."

I stifled a wince at the grandparents comment. Gah. Why did forty suddenly feel old?

"You have a good day," Ron said.

She gave us a little wave and walked out the door.

By now, I was impatient.

"Okay Ron. Spill."

"I think I saw Petunia's cat. Or a cat just like it."

"What? Where? Do you think Sapphire was out all night?"

He shook his head.

"She was in a cat carrier, head poking out the top."

Now I was confused.

"What? Just sitting on the sidewalk?"

Now Ron looked irritated.

"No. That's what I'm trying to tell you! The carrier was strapped to the back of one of those electric bikes everyone's riding these days. Though what's wrong with good old pedal power, I don't know."

"First off, not everyone has the muscles or energy, and second..." I snapped myself out of a building rant about accessibility. "Did you see who was riding the bike?"

He frowned. "I didn't. But whatever shirt or jacket they had on kind of sparkled."

"Sparkled like reflective biking gear? Or sparkled like sequins and rhinestones?"

"Sparkled like one of those shirts or jackets people

used to wear to raves. The ones that kind of look like an oil slick running across your back and chest."

I knew those shirts well. I'd made a short-lived attempt to be cool in my late 20s, before I settled into what John sometimes called my "visiting professor" style.

"That could be anyone," I said, looking at Ron.

"That's the problem, isn't it?"

But in a sea of dance party lovers, how did we figure out who it was?

CHAPTER 11

Marsha

"WE HAVE TO HURRY, KLAUS!"

We were back on the sidewalk. Garrett carried our new toys safely in his backpack.

"What now?" Klaus whined, stopping to sniff the corner of Ron's building. I didn't blame him. Ron's building was full of interesting smells. But we didn't have time for that. Not today.

"You heard Fred! He said the bicycle with Sapphire on it was heading the direction of the river, not the hills!"

"So?"

I barked in irritation. Klaus was sweet, but gah, sometimes he needed to pay better attention.

"So, we need to explore that way! Do something to convince Garrett we need to head that way!"

"On it."

Klaus immediately changed direction, looking back at Garrett, tugging at his leash. His tongue lolled out in his "I'm such a cute and fluffy, happy dog. You can deny me nothing" look.

"Where do you want to go?" Garrett asked. "I guess we

could walk down that way. I want to stop into Maddy's Candles and Curios anyway. See if she has anything interesting outside. Maybe I'll get John a concentration candle or something."

Sucker. I gave Klaus an admiring look. He might not be as smart as I am, but he's good at convincing humans to do what he wants.

We trotted along, pausing to sniff on occasion. Trouble was, it was sometimes hard to smell cats close to the ground. They tended to like walls and fence tops, and we just don't reach that high. And if it really was Sapphire on that bicycle? How were we supposed to catch a scent at all?

Klaus and I wove around people's legs. It wasn't as crowded on the sidewalk as the day before. Most people were at work, like John was this morning. He usually took his day off when Garrett had the shop closed, but sometimes he had "things on the calendar" that he needed to attend to.

I understand that. Some days I really need to go to Bruiser's or Fred's. Other days, I really need an extra nap.

There was a tug on my leash. I paused and looked back. Klaus stood stock still, nose quivering, ears alert.

"What'd you find, boy?" Garrett asked.

I trotted over. *"Smell something?"*

"Not sure." Klaus's eyes were trained on a small Victorian house set back from the street. It had one of those billowing gardens I loved to get lost in. It was like a corgi-sized jungle filled with flowers. Pink. Red. Yellow. Purple. They all waved in a slight breeze and smelled really good.

"I love this place," I said. *"But John and Garrett never let us enter people's yards, so I don't know why you stopped here."*

"I'm not sure either," Klaus replied. *"Something made me stop, but now I can't figure out what."*

We both looked around and sniffed at the entrance to the walkway that led to the purple door. A human face peered out from behind lace curtains, then disappeared.

I glanced at Garrett to make sure he was okay with us stopping here. He was scrolling through something on his phone. Good. That should occupy him for a bit.

"Cover me," I said to Klaus. *"I'm going in."*

He parked his butt on the sidewalk, right next to Garrett's feet. Good tactic. If Garrett realized something was wrong, he'd have to get around Klaus first. Maybe Klaus is smarter than I give him credit for.

At any rate, now it was my turn. I acted casual, just sniffing along, making my way up the walkway that ran through the garden. I sniffed a toad crouching in a little ceramic pot a few feet into the flowers. I smelled water from a birdbath on one side, and a small water feature contained in a big basin filled with rocks. The water fountained and burbled, and was surrounded by ferns. It looked like a very nice place to rest on a hot day. I bet the toad liked it.

I was kept slowly pulling on my retractable leash, glancing back to make sure Garrett hadn't noticed yet. Nope. Still looking at his phone. Klaus panted at me, a goofy grin on his face. He loved these assignments as much as I do.

I was trying to decide whether to make a run at the purple door when it opened and an ancient man peaked out. His skin was dark, his cheeks and chin stubbled with silver that matched his curling, thinning hair. He wore those soft pants I like to snuggle with, and a faded, worn-out T-shirt that looked as thin as the tight curls on his head. He pushed the glasses up on his nose and smiled.

"Come to visit, little dog?"

"Marsha! What have I told you about going into people's gardens?" Garrett made his way up the walkway, trailed by Klaus.

Uh oh. I was trapped between Garrett and the old man now.

I barked.

"That's all right. She doesn't mean any harm, I'm sure." The old man stepped out onto his little porch and shut the door. "I'm always pleased when people want to admire my garden."

He lowered himself onto the blue chair and patted his knees. "Come say hello, pretty girl."

I preened a bit, then climbed the three steps and nosed his shins. The old man reached down to pat my head softly, then looked up at Garrett.

"Her name is Marsha, you say?"

Klaus scaled the steps, which took a bit of effort. His legs are shorter than mine.

"Marsha P. Johnson," Garrett replied. I could hear the smile in his voice. "And this one's Klaus Nomi."

"Marsha P. Johnson. A true hero. Pity how she died. And Klaus Nomi?" The man shook his head. "Never did care for his music, but I can't deny he was talented. Lost too many good people in those days."

He peered at Garrett. "It's good to keep memories alive. I'm glad you chose their names for these two sweethearts."

He scratched Klaus's head. Klaus looked up at the old man in adoring doggy bliss.

"My name is Garrett, by the way."

"I'm Charles. Charles Johnson. Pleased to meet you. You'll forgive me for not offering you something to drink, but by the time I get into the kitchen and back, I'm sure these two will be on their way."

"It's a beautiful garden you have here," Garrett said.

"Yes. Yes. It was my late partner's pride and joy. Now it's my memory garden. See those steppingstones?"

He pointed. We all looked through the flowers. Sure enough, there were decorated round step stones with tile and glass marbles in the concrete. And what looked like names.

"Those are all important people, now gone. I should make a stone for Marsha P., now that I think of it."

"But Marsha is still alive!" Klaus barked.

"He means the person I'm named after, silly."

"That's really beautiful," Garrett said. "But this garden seems like a lot to keep up."

"Oh, it is. But I have help now. My nephew moved in with me six months ago. He's a good boy. Taking classes at the university there." He gestured in the general direction of the river. I knew the university. Sometimes John and Garrett took us there to run around.

"Hey, Charles," Garrett said. "Have you seen any animals wandering around, looking lost?"

Charles thought a moment, then shook his head. "Some animals missing from their homes?"

"It appears so. Petunia from the flower shop is missing her cat, and someone else lost their hamster."

"Flower Frenzy, down the way? That's a shame. She's a nice gal."

The door opened again, and a dark-skinned young Black man poked his head out.

"Uncle Charles, you okay with a salad for lunch? Tuna?" He stopped, staring at all of us. "Oh. Hello."

"I'm Garrett." Garrett held out his hand to shake.

The younger man hesitated, then held his hand out, too. "Xavier."

"Well, we'd best leave you to it," Garrett said. "Nice to meet you, Charles. Xavier."

"Come back any time to visit," Charles said, slowly pushing himself up from the chair. "I'm almost always home."

I wasn't ready to leave yet, and I could tell Klaus wasn't, either. There was still too much to explore. But when humans wanted to leave, sometimes you just couldn't stop them.

Soon enough, we were back on the sidewalk. When we got to the edge of the garden, Klaus stopped. I bumped into his butt and his tail thwapped my nose.

"What are you doing?" I asked.

"Come on, you two. Time to head home for lunch."

Klaus sniffed the air, then looked out at the street.

"You see that?"

I looked.

Klaus trundled toward the sidewalk's edge and started barking.

"What, Klaus?" Garrett asked.

"Tracks! Tracks! Tracks!"

I headed toward his side and looked down. Sure enough, it looked like a bicycle had skidded to a stop in the street. Right here.

Klaus ran back to where Charles's garden bumped against the fence marking the yard next door. He sniffed excitedly. I noticed Garrett was taking pictures of the tire tracks with his phone.

"What is it?" I asked.

"I smell a cat! It climbed this fence!"

We both looked at each other, then turned to Garrett and started barking frantically.

"Sapphire is free! She's on the loose!"

Garrett crouched down to talk to us, a serious look on his face. "I really wish you could speak human. You're right, there's something suspicious about those tire tracks."

He was actually listening! Good human!

Klaus gave a swift bark, then led Garrett to the fence and pawed at the boards.

Garrett looked more closely, then reached out and pinched something between his fingers.

When he held it up to the sun shining through the trees, I saw what he'd found.

It was a tuft of silvery gray fur.

CHAPTER 12
Garrett

"SAPPHIRE," I said, holding the silver fur up. "It has to be."

I peered into the yard next Charles's. Where his was a riot of color, fragrance, and sound, the small yard behind its neat wood fence looked almost sterile. A dogwood tree sat in the center of a patch of perfectly mown grass in front of a cute little white Victorian bungalow, clearly the cousin to Charles's, but with a staid, black door. Some flowers from Charles's cottage garden poked their heads through the fence, and I just bet seed pods swarmed past the barrier every year.

I smiled. Whoever lived in this tidy home probably cursed the old man every spring. Frankly, I preferred the semi-wild garden to this overly tame edition. Looking down the length of the fence, toward the backyards, I saw more trees. Looked like some fruit trees. Cherry and maybe fig or persimmon.

Plenty of places for a cat to hide. But a pampered, indoor cat like Sapphire? I wasn't sure how long she would last outside. We really needed to mount a search. Maybe I could ask whoever lived here to check.

"Come on, you two. Let's head in. But behave yourselves."

Neither Klaus nor Marsha replied, but they trotted obediently enough as I opened the latch on the gate and headed up the walk. The little wooden gate was strange. Most Portland homes didn't bother enclosing the whole front yard, not unless they had dogs. But I saw no sign of an animal. No dropped toys. No piles of poop, either. And nothing barked at us as we got closer to that black door.

Any self-respecting dog would be barking their head off about now, with a strange human and two strange dogs approaching. I don't care how quiet and well behaved a dog is, there are some things that are too insulting to bear. Like dogs in your yard that you hadn't invited.

Not that I was much different. If left to my own devices, I'd curl up in our house and never leave, let alone invite people inside. Luckily, John was more gregarious and pushed me out of my comfort zone.

All the time.

I mounted the little porch. "Stay back a little, okay? We don't know if they have any pets. Sit."

Klaus and Marsha both plopped their butts down. I knocked. We all waited.

No one answered. I knocked again, just in case they were old like Charles next door and needed extra time.

Finally, I had to admit defeat.

"Okay. Let's go to Petunia's."

She would want to know there was a possible Sapphire sighting. I texted John to tell him where I was headed and not to expect me home just yet.

Keep me posted, he texted back.

I clicked for the dogs, and the three of us headed toward Flower Frenzy.

As we approached the shop, I grew concerned. She was usually open on Mondays, at least I thought so. Petunia always said Mondays and Fridays were her two best days.

"Friday because people are hoping to get a little romance," she once told me, "and Monday to apologize for being an ass over the weekend."

There was no sandwich board out front, and the flower-painted sign in the door read "closed." The towering, sculptural window displays blocked part of my view, making it hard to see into the store, but I thought I saw movement. Petunia? Or an intruder?

I banged on the glass front door and waited. Marsha barked.

There was a rustling, then the chunk of the heavy locks releasing. Petunia poked her head around the edge of the door.

She looked terrible. Her wig was askew, and her makeup was mostly gone. She looked like she'd been crying. An extra-large bag of cool ranch tortilla chips was in one hand, and I saw pasty white dust stuck to what was left of her pink lipstick.

"Garrett," she said. "Oh Garrett. Thank goodness you're here!"

She opened the door wide enough for us to enter, then shut and bolted it again.

"Come on back," she said, her fuzzy slippers slapping against the black and white checkerboard floor.

Wow. I had never seen Petunia looking this way, not even when I'd delivered chicken soup for her while she was sick. But if anything happened to Marsha or Klaus? I'd probably be in bad shape, too.

The dogs sniffed a bit but didn't complain when I tugged on their leashes. We all trooped toward the back, past a curtain beaded so when it hung straight, it looked like a large peony. One of John's favorite flowers.

Which reminded me, I never did get him the promised bouquet. Clearly today was not the day for it, either. I'd never been in the back of Flower Frenzy before and was surprised at how light and bright it was. Most back-of-shop spaces trend toward the dim and slightly disorganized and dingy, but not Petunia's place.

Windows were set high in the back walls, and a large green table commanded the center of the room. White walls bounced the light around. Dried flowers hung from pegboards, ready to be made into seasonal wreaths, and other supplies clumped in neat categories on a set of floating shelves.

A long counter with an old zinc sink ran along one wall, with cabinets beneath painted the same green as the worktable.

"Petunia, this place is impressive."

She looked around, as if seeing it for the first time. "I suppose it is. Thank you."

She slumped in a wood chair at the table, and I took another, wondering how to help her. If we were at my place, now would be the time to fix Petunia a comforting cup of tea. Instead, I shifted in my chair and cleared my throat as Klaus and Marsha snuffled around the room, exploring.

If Petunia hadn't been so out of it, she would've asked me what the heck was wrong with me.

"Petunia, I, uh…"

She looked up at me, finally seeing my face. "Why did you come? Is it Sapphire?"

There was no easy way to tell a person that their prized cat was probably sleeping rough and eating who knows what.

"I think Sapphire escaped from whoever took her. I think she's in the neighborhood somewhere. There's a yard she might be in, but when I knocked, no one was home."

She shot up, knocking her chair back. "We have to go. Now. Poor Sapphire must be so scared!"

"I think we should call our friends and ask everyone to be on the lookout," I said. "That will be more efficient than you and I traipsing around on our own."

Marsha barked, *"We need to organize the dogs!"*

"Yes! Yes!" Klaus said. *"Bruiser and Fred!"*

Petunia gave the corgis a watery smile. "It's almost as if you want to help, don't you, babies?"

"Of course we do!" Marsha replied.

"They are pretty smart," I said, smiling down at my two best friends. Other than John, of course. "And they like you."

"Well," Petunia said, "I'll gladly accept their help. And yours, Garrett. Thank you. Now, where do we start?"

"I'll head home and start making phone calls. And maybe I can talk to people on my way."

I stood, feeling a bit better that Petunia had the latest news, and that we at least had the beginnings of a plan. I still didn't know what to do about Sparkle Toes and Mr. Cheeks, though.

And I wasn't sure I trusted Petunia to not go climbing fences herself once I was gone. She had a glint in her eye. That was better than the defeated grief, but it also worried me a bit.

"You want to come home with me?" I asked. "You can

help tell me who to call, and then you can eat dinner with John and me."

She looked around the room, then down at herself, as if just realizing her hair was a mess and she wore house slippers.

"Let me meet you in an hour or two. I need to get cleaned up. And I'm not feeling very hungry."

Petunia definitely needed to eat, but I had learned the hard way to not push people. Just because I thought I knew what was best didn't mean they would agree.

"All right," I said. "But you'll come, right? You won't do anything foolish?"

Like searching for your cat alone?

She looked at me, hands on her skinny hips. "Now Garrett, have I ever done a foolish thing in my life?"

I knew better than to answer that question. But I was worried all the same.

When a person answers a question with another question?

It means they don't want to lie.

CHAPTER 13
Marsha

GARRETT DECIDED to head home directly, but Klaus and I both tugged him toward Bruiser's. We really needed to get all the dogs on the case. I wished there was a way to get Fred back to Bruiser's, too. But since I don't have a phone, I couldn't just text him, the way Garrett was texting John right now.

Besides, my paws just mash a bunch of buttons at once. I know. I tried on John's phone once when he set it on the coffee table. A siren went off and made John mad.

How was I supposed to know that would happen?

"You're back!" Bruiser lumbered to his feet and sniffed me in greeting. Which meant he snuffled, snorted, and then wiped drool all over me. Kind of gross. I'd mentioned the problem once and really hurt the bulldog's feelings, so now I just cleaned myself as well as I could when he wasn't looking.

I loved Bruiser and not hurting him was worth the extra effort.

"We have news!" Klaus barked, after his own round of sniffing. Klaus didn't seem to mind the drool like I did. He

also had a bigger dog-crush on Bruiser than I did, which was fine.

Garrett looked up from his phone and realized he still held our leashes. He quickly secured us to one of the little rings at a table nearby.

"John should be here any minute," he said. "You three be good. No harassing toddlers this time!"

"Hey!" I barked. *"Not fair! That baby was attacking Klaus!"*

"She really was," Klaus woofed.

Garrett just gave us a stern look and headed back inside Bruiser's Best Beans. I hoped he brought us a toasted sandwich with ham and cheese. Those things are delicious, even if they do make Klaus fart something terrible. Toasted sandwiches are totally worth it.

"So," Bruiser said, thumping back down on the ground. *"What's the news?"*

I noticed he had reddish blotches on the white parts of his fur. Must be from all the dropped cherries he was laying on. I nosed a few of the ruby orbs away to clear a space for myself and lay down next to him.

"We found a tuft of Sapphire's fur!" Klaus barked. He quivered with excitement, still standing up.

Bruiser raised his head.

"At least, we think it is Sapphire's. We're not sure yet. But we need your help!" I barked.

"What can I do?"

"We need you to talk to Fred next time Ron comes by. Ron and Fred saw Sapphire on the back of a bicycle, and there were bicycle tracks near where we found the fur."

"We think Sapphire escaped!"

"Escaped from Petunia?" The furrows in Bruiser's face got even deeper.

"No," I said. *"Escaped from the person who stole her!"*

"Hey there, Klaus and Marsha! Is Garrett inside?" John had arrived. He bent down to give us skritches. He was wearing a loose white shirt and relaxed trousers with sandals. For a human, he looked pretty nice.

"Yes!" I barked. *"And we want toasted sandwiches!"*

"Hey there, Bruiser." John scratched the bulldog's head before standing again. "See you all in a minute."

Bruiser snorted. Not at John. Sometimes that's just how Bruiser breathes.

"What makes you think it was Sapphire's fur?" he asked.

I put my head on my paws, thinking. Bruiser just waited, while Klaus lapped noisily at a metal bowl of water.

"Well," I said. *"It was gray, or silver, but I guess it could have belonged to another cat. But Ron said he and Fred saw a cat that looked like Sapphire on the back of a bicycle last night. In a carrier."*

"And we think she bravely escaped!" Klaus yipped.

"Wow," Bruiser said. *"Escaping from a carrier? That takes gumption."*

We all pondered that for a moment while we waited for Garrett and John to come back. Soon enough, the scent of toasted ham and cheese reached my sensitive nose. Yes! Even if I didn't get a whole sandwich, a cheesy crust and bit of ham was likely in my future.

Which reminded me... I wondered if anyone had checked with the psychic on the street. I mean, corgis don't believe in seeing the future—why would we want to, when the present is so interesting?—but talking with Adam the ghost made me think there was more to life than what was in front of my nose.

Garrett carried two sandwiches and some little dog

treats that smelled like ham, while John had napkins and big glasses of iced tea. We all shot to our feet as they approached, and Garrett laughed.

"Smell your treats, do you? Just let me set this stuff down."

He set down the sandwiches with their side of chips. Yum. Crunchy fried potatoes. John slid onto one of the benches and Garrett gave us each a cookie.

I took mine delicately, my teeth barely touching it, and settled in to chew. Bruiser was already done with his treat and crumbs were flying from Klaus's mouth. Yep. They were definitely ham cookies. But that didn't mean I wouldn't be eyeing the sandwiches, too. Maybe we'd all get double treats this afternoon.

"Should I call Ron?" Garrett was saying, once both men had taken their first bites. They must have started talking inside.

"Seems like a good idea. What time does he close on Mondays?"

I pricked up my ears as Garrett checked his watch.

"Early, I think. Maybe around four? Maybe we could invite him over for dinner."

"*Yes!*" I barked. "*That is a very good idea! Fred can come, too!*"

"*Fred goes everywhere with Ron,*" Klaus pointed out. That was true. We were only part-time shop dogs, but Fred worked every day Ron did. I suppose some restaurants and nightclubs might not let the old black lab in, but otherwise, Klaus was right.

Where Ron was, Fred was sure to be, too.

"*How are you going to figure out if it's Sapphire or not?*" Bruiser asked.

"*That's what we need to figure out, I guess.*" I thought

some more. *"But be on the lookout when Bex and Jacki take you for your walks, okay? We'll try to stop by every day to share information."*

Hopefully, tonight we'd talk to Fred. He saw every animal in the neighborhood in the store. All the animals who went outside, at least. If anyone could get the word out about Sapphire, Fred could.

The only way to find out who that tuft of gray fur belonged to? Was to start looking in as many places as we could.

And human noses just weren't good enough for the job.

CHAPTER 14

Garrett

I WAS STARTING to regret this plan. Big time. Even Marsha seemed disgruntled.

We were trooping along the sidewalks of the neighborhood, surrounded by drag queens, dykes on bicycles—no electric bikes, though. I checked—and an assortment of other queers, young to old. Everyone who had a dog had brought them, and the excited barking only added to the circus-like atmosphere.

No self-respecting cat was going to come out into the hullabaloo. And a frightened cat? Would run the other direction. John was his usual placid self. I guess killing people for a living meant a little thing like searching for a lost cat wasn't that big a deal.

"This is a disaster," I muttered.

Ron, who was walking just behind me with Fred, laughed. "It most certainly is. We should have known better than to tell folks to bring their friends. Sapphire is probably hiding under a porch somewhere, waiting for things to quiet down."

"So, what do we do?" John asked, right as Sweetheart Digs sashayed up in his too-tight black pants and white sequined blazer, and those ubiquitous sunglasses. Vyviane was right behind him, dressed in loose white trousers tied with a scarf, and a white sleeveless blouse. Her blonde hair fanned out around her head and she wore dark glasses, so I couldn't see her eyes.

At least she had the good graces to hang back a bit today. She must have felt me glaring.

Or maybe she knew Marsha would bite her. Or John would. My partner had some choice words to say about Vyviane lately. But I also knew he couldn't stand Sweetheart Digs. They had some sort of history, but John hadn't told me the story yet. Every time I thought to ask, something more important came up.

Sweetheart drew his dark sunglasses down his nose with one white finger. He had a little candy heart tattooed on his pinky finger. It looked new. If he wasn't so obnoxious, I would have to admit that his blue eyes were quite lovely.

"What is your plan? As mayor, I'm happy to provide any direction the people need. And this—" Sweetheart Digs waved a hand around "—lacks direction."

"You aren't the mayor," John growled.

Well, scratch the thought that my love is placid. He looked ready to kill right now, just like a Big Bad in one of his novels.

John's growl just made Sweetheart Digs' smile grow wider, flashing his blinding veneers. The guy really thought he was in Hollywood or something.

And I was tired of dealing with him. And tired of the noise and the crowd. Did I mention I get easily overwhelmed? Yeah. I was heading toward overwhelm. I could feel my brain racing, about to shut down, and sweat beaded on my upper lip. I hated sweating.

"I'm calling this off," I said. "It's not working. We're just scaring Sapphire off."

"But what about Petunia?" Sweetheart asked.

We all looked her way. Her makeup and hair were perfect, and she wore a vintage 1960s hot pink and lime green pantsuit. She waved a pristine handkerchief near her face, as if she could burst into tears at any moment. But the look on her face was studied. Petunia was having the time of her life, basking in everyone's attention.

Where had the grief-stricken cat owner of a few hours ago gone?

"Take her to get a drink. Say you're there to console her," I said. "Thank everyone for helping."

"And what are you going to do, while I keep everyone entertained?" Sweetheart asked. I was about to answer when I noticed Vyviane staring at me. She quickly looked away but was still within listening distance.

I didn't trust either of them. John gave my fingers a quick squeeze, then dropped my hand. Message received.

"We're going home to design fliers. We'll get the neighborhood to look for Sapphire as they're walking around. The crowd must be scaring her."

"If Sapphire is loose at all," Sweetheart Digs replied, sliding his glasses back into place.

"Right. If Sapphire is loose at all." I stared straight into those stupid dark glasses, and he finally looked away.

Back to Vyviane.

When he turned back, the smile was on his face again. "Okay, then. I'll do my part. Civic leadership and all that."

I wanted to punch him. Another sign I was getting overwhelmed. Too much stimulation makes modulating my emotions difficult. But as John likes to remind me, my hands aren't built for punching.

And neither is the rest of me.

Sweetheart Digs didn't seem to notice my animosity, though he had to feel it radiating off of John.

He turned, clapped his hands, then put his fingers in his mouth to let out a piercing whistle.

"Okay, everybody! We've decided to call this off for now. Let's all go get a drink!"

The crowd cheered. Petunia looked a bit put out until Sweetheart Digs put an arm around her shoulders and whispered something in her ear. She nodded, and they slowly walked away, trailed closely by Vyviane.

The motley crowd moved with them.

"What do you think those three are up to?" Ron asked quietly.

I jumped. I'd forgotten my big friend was there.

"I don't know," John answered. "But I don't trust any of them all of a sudden. Including Petunia."

I looked from John to Ron, then down at the three dogs.

"*Let's go!*" Marsha barked.

"Okay," I said. "Let's patrol and see if these three can sniff out one gray cat."

"Once the crowd clears," Ron agreed.

He was right. People still milled about, having conversations. Nothing ever happened quickly in Pride Street, especially not on a warm and pleasant early summer evening.

"First, let's go back to my store," he said. "There's something I want to show you."

"Lead on," I said.

CHAPTER 15
Marsha

"DID YOU FIND SOMETHING?" I barked at Fred as we sauntered down the street.

We had to dodge the people who'd come out to help find Sapphire. People still clogged the sidewalks with bicycles and strollers, and three people on roller skates laughed loudly as they did tricks in the street. Humans. How they thought any of this would help find a cat was beyond me. If only Garrett and John had listened to us... we would have just sent out a handful of dogs to do the job.

Humans get distracted too easily, I think. Especially when it's sunny out. And they tease dogs about our "squirrel!" reflex. They don't understand the danger squirrels pose, do they?

"Ron thinks he did," Fred replied. He wasn't quick about anything, and I'd learned to wait for a response. *"But I'm not sure."*

A clump of people stood yakking in front of Bones, Dogs, and Harmony. Ron pushed his way through with a smile and got out his keys.

"Hey, brother! You opening? You got the new press from Preytorians?" one of the men asked Ron.

Ron shook his head. "Sorry, friend. Come back tomorrow. Tuesday is my drop off day. It should be in then!"

Once inside the store, Ron flipped on some lights. It was much quieter in here than on the street. Cooler, too.

Josephine Baker gave a squawk from inside her big covered cage. Ron clucked at her, and the cage grew quiet again.

"What did you want to show us?" Garrett asked.

I wanted to know, too.

"Just give me a minute," he said, and started rustling around behind the counter.

"What is it?" I asked Fred.

The old black lab just looked at me and turned his graying nose back to Ron.

Guess that meant I should shut up and wait. But waiting is hard. I wanted to do something. If Mr. Cheeks was dead and Sapphire was missing or gone rogue, did that mean the rest of us were in danger?

"Klaus?"

"Yes?" My friend was distracted by a shiny toy display on the countertop, his furry little neck craned up to see.

"Do you think we should be worried?"

"About Sapphire?"

"About us."

He dropped his chin and gave me a shocked look.

"You think someone will steal us?" he barked in alarm. *"Should we tell Garrett and John? How will we protect ourselves? Can I bite someone?"*

Great. Now he was frantic, practically turning in circles, and barking his head off.

"Sshh! Klaus! What has gotten into you!" John admonished.

Klaus whimpered. I was about to reply when Ron found what he was searching for.

He came up with a small plastic bag. The kind Garrett sometimes got vintage jewelry in for his store. He didn't sell much of that sort of thing, but enough that I'd seen those little bags before.

Ron held the bag up so we could see. Something glinted inside. Two things.

John and Garrett leaned closer.

"I want to see!" I barked.

"It's an earring and one of those sequin thingies," Fred replied. *"Ron showed me earlier."*

Oh. More human stuff. Why hadn't Fred just said that before?

I turned to the lab. *"You were holding out on clues?"*

Fred whuffed. *"Didn't think it was important."*

"Is that another earring?" John was asking.

"And a silver sequin," Ron replied. "I found them just inside the door, off to one side, when I was closing. Almost missed them, except a couple of dogs tracked in a lot of dirt today, so I was giving an extra good sweep and mop to the place."

Garrett held the bag now. "They were next to each other?"

Ron leaned against the countertop, his long coiled locs dangling over his shoulder. "No. But close enough."

"I don't understand the significance," John said. "I mean, I know there was that other missing earring, but people in this neighborhood shed bling right and left. These could belong to anyone."

"But Ron would have seen them!" I barked.

"Didn't you see anyone who came in wearing sequins?" Garrett asked. Good. He must have heard me.

Ron sighed. "That's what worries me. I didn't. I mean, we get characters in all the time, right? That's just the neighborhood. But I didn't get anyone like that in the store today."

"How about in the last week?" John asked.

Ron crossed his arms over his chest and looked out the front windows. The crowd was finally thinning out, which meant we might be able to explore before going home.

"Nah, man. I swept and mopped on Saturday and haven't seen anyone like that since then."

"Sweetheart Digs has a sequined blazer!" I said to Fred and Klaus.

"But what about the earring?" Klaus asked. *"And what about Sapphire and Mr. Cheeks?"*

Klaus was right. The earring and sequins may have looked like clues, but we needed to focus.

"So, how do you think they got in here?" Garrett asked.

"I think someone came in after I closed. Here. Follow me."

Fred rose from his bed and led us down the aisle, as if he knew exactly what Ron wanted to show us. I looked and looked and didn't see anything that seemed unusual, except Ron needed to restock his cat treats.

"See that?" he pointed. We all looked. I even sniffed around the area where he was pointing.

"You smell anything off?" I asked Klaus.

"No. Just liver treats and tuna. Think we can eat dinner soon?"

"You already had food at Bruiser's!"

"But that wasn't dinner!"

"You're such a puppy!"

"All right, you two," Garrett said. "Play nice."

I growled, but kept it soft, which meant Garrett could ignore it. That was our arrangement. As long as I pretended to not growl or bark, he let me get away with it.

"Cat treats are missing," Fred said. *"And some food. That's what Ron is pointing at."*

I saw it then. Where the stock seemed a bit thin? There was an empty space on the shelf where something should be.

"I don't see it," John said.

"Cat treats are gone," Ron said, "along with some food and litter. I think someone broke in and stole stuff, but they were neat about it, so I didn't notice at first."

"Stolen treats!" Klaus barked. *"That's terrible!"*

"You're right, my friend," Ron said to Klaus. "I'm not happy about it, either."

"But if someone broke in, it must have been last night, right? And isn't that when you saw the cat on the bicycle?"

Good questions, Garrett.

Ron stopped. "I guess that's right."

"Does that mean the gray fur didn't belong to Sapphire?" John asked Garrett. "You think someone is still holding her hostage? Or that there's a team?"

The humans all looked at each other. No one said anything.

Finally, Garrett sighed and scrubbed at his face the way he only does when he's tired or overwhelmed. He's like Klaus that way. Sometimes Klaus gets really barky or grumpy when there's too much stimulation.

"I don't know what to think anymore," Garrett said. "But I'm suddenly exhausted. Can we look for Sapphire tomorrow before we open?"

"Yeah, man," Ron replied. "Let's do that. Besides, even

if Sapphire is still out there, there's no way we're coaxing her out of hiding tonight. Not after all that ridiculousness."

"Let's get you home, babe," John said.

I looked at Fred. The old lab looked back.

"Fred, if people are coming in your store at night, do you think Josephine Baker would know? Or would she sleep right through it?"

She had barely made a peep when we came in, but that's because Ron reassured her right away.

Fred sniffed. *"I can ask her in the morning when Ron takes the blanket off her cage. But sometimes she just screams at me."*

Fair enough. But at least Fred would try.

"Can we go home and eat now?" Klaus whined.

I was filled with energy and still wanted to hunt for Sapphire, the way we had all agreed, but that wasn't happening.

Maybe Adam would have some ideas. I bet that ghost had seen a lot of things when he was alive.

CHAPTER 16
Adam

THIS MYSTERY WAS A PUZZLE, and not one I'd dealt with while I was alive.

Missing animals? I guess it must have happened, though we were more concerned with fighting government health agencies for care and keeping each other alive. Who had time for things like stealing other people's pets?

I looked around the house, remembering Lucy, who used to happily snore next to the fireplace in winter, sleeping on a little mat right where Marsha and Klaus's living room bed was. She and I didn't share the big main bedroom, like Garrett and John, though. As a matter of fact, my space was the small bedroom that was now John's office. A writer. What a great job.

I worked construction during the day. Hard, physical labor, but I loved it.

Until I got too sick to work at all. I remained proud of the work my friends and I did to try to change the tide of that illness and make people pay attention to the fact that just because we were gay, didn't mean we all deserved to die.

From what I've heard from Garrett and John's conversations, things these days sometimes look better on the surface, but I see the way Garrett's face gets pinched sometimes. He's worried about the state of the world. And being trans, I supposed he would be. The world isn't always kind to people it considers oddballs and freaks.

And sometimes you just have to say, "screw that" and live your life as best you can. That's all anyone can do on this planet, right? Make life a bit better for yourself and the people around you. And if you have the energy, fight for things larger than yourself, as well.

So, while I didn't understand the pettiness of stealing someone's animal companion when there were more important things going on, I sympathized with the people who were left bereft.

I crouched by the dog bed, staring down at the two resting corgis. They both had their eyes closed, but I didn't think they were asleep.

::What did you find out?::

Marsha startled in her bed, jostling Klaus, who cracked an eye open.

"Adam," he woofed in a soft greeting.

Marsha perked up and raised her head. *"It's been a long day, and I'm so frustrated I want to bite."*

I sat on the floor and crossed my legs. It was a little funny, positioning myself as a ghost. I had to relearn what my body shape was supposed to be doing, now that it was the memory of solid form. But it felt comforting to do the things that felt "normal" for an embodied person, so I learned again to walk, and sit, and move my arms, and cross my legs.

I wish I could get back the feel of a man's neck under

my hand as I drew his face in for a kiss. But I supposed we can't have everything we want.

::So, no new clues?::

Marsha sat up, tilting her glossy dark head in thought.

I tried to lean against the coffee table, but started to sink into the wood, so sat up straight again myself.

"That's the thing," Marsha replied. *"There are new clues, but they're only making everything more confusing!"*

::Talk it through.::

That was what we always did, my friends and I, when faced with an insurmountable problem. We talked, then we strategized, then we settled on tactics. That's how we shut down the new light rail system two blocks from City Hall. People weren't listening to the concerns of a bunch of queers before that point, but they sure did after.

"Well…" Marsha began.

"Ron found another earring! And a sequin! And Garrett found a tuft of Sapphire's fur!"

::Really? Those all seem like solid clues.::

"Yes," Marsha woofed. *"Except someone also stole cat treats from Ron's, and we don't know if that was before or after whatever cat that left that gray fur leapt the fence."*

I stroked my mustache. *::You mean there's more than one missing cat? And how about the hamster?::*

Marsha's little black brow furrowed, causing the two brown spots above her eyes to dip toward each other.

"I still think Mr. Cheeks is dead, but I can't be sure because we didn't find a body. And Sapphire? Klaus and I will look for a gray cat wandering around tomorrow because it looked like she escaped from the back of a bicycle. But," she sighed, and lay back down with a thump, *"none of it makes sense anymore."*

We all sat quietly for a while. I heard the refrigerator turn over in the kitchen, and John's and Garrett's voices came softly from upstairs. They were probably having this very discussion while getting ready for bed.

::Sometimes when things don't make any sense, I try to look at it from another angle. Or listen differently. Think the unthinkable thought.::

"How does a person think an unthinkable thought?" Klaus barked.

::They try to think in a way they've never thought before. They entertain a thought that seems ridiculous, and then see if it starts to make sense.::

That's what you did when you had no other choices left. Entertain the ridiculous because what seemed logical wasn't working anymore.

Marsha looked at me with big, dark, doggie eyes.

"Maybe Sapphire and Mr. Cheeks aren't really missing after all."

And that was a thought worth contemplating. Because if the animals weren't really missing?

Something else was going on. And it likely wasn't good.

CHAPTER 17

Garrett

YARROW MOPED around the store in their rainbow shoes, black jeans, and black T-shirt with a golden beehive on the front. It read "All we have is each other."

Wasn't that the truth?

They paused in front of a dramatic Art Deco era mirror over an inlaid wood Deco dresser, and leaned in to examine their reflection, patting their short, bright yellow cap of curls that contrasted beautifully with their rich brown skin.

"None of this makes any sense," they said to their reflection.

"Not so far," I said, my mind half on the conversation and half on the mood board on my computer screen. I stood behind the long front counter, trying to settle on color swatches for a new design job I was hoping to land. The design part of Dandy Decor and Designs was starting to take off. I'd recently done a few jobs for satisfied customers who just happened to have friends with money and not enough time or taste to design their homes themselves.

Not that I only designed for rich people. I made sure to have some smaller packages for folks who want to refresh their tiny studio rentals. I was there once and wanted to give back. But frankly? It was the high-end jobs that paid rent on the storefront and my part of the mortgage on our house. I was inching closer to making as much as John, but not yet.

Luckily, we weren't one of those couples who competed over stuff like money. As a matter of fact, we didn't compete at all. That's why John had been so amazing for me. We were actually friends and companions who wanted to support each other's dreams.

Yarrow sauntered toward me on their long, black denim clad legs. I did not have long legs. As a matter of fact, at five foot seven, I'm used to being surrounded by people taller than I am.

"I mean," Yarrow continued, "you found that fur, but then Ron said he'd been robbed? And all they stole was cat food and some salmon treats?"

I nodded, distracted, and slid a mossy green onto my mood board. Was that better for the design? Or would an emerald green work? If it were just up to me, I'd go with emerald. I love saturated colors. But some clients preferred more muted shades of color. And luckily, no one who looked at my portfolio and followed through with hiring me wanted all white anything.

"Garrett? Are you listening to me?"

"I'm listening, Yarrow. But I also have to work." Which was useless. I turned toward the younger nonbinary pansexual in front of me and smiled. Yarrow was good people, and still finding their way in the world. It wouldn't hurt me to take some time to listen.

Besides, people were still counting on me to get to the

bottom of this case, which was getting murkier by the minute.

The bells above the front door chimed, and both of us turned. I pasted a smile on my face to greet the newcomer, but the corners of my mouth fell when I saw who it was.

"Hello Sweetheart, what brings you in?"

He gave me a slight frown, smoothing his dark brown hair even though it was already perfect.

Oops. A frown wasn't good. I'd kept my voice polite, but probably shouldn't have said that last part.

He shucked off those dark glasses he always wore, flicking his eyes from me to Yarrow, and back again. "I'm here to see if you'd found out anything about Sapphire. I just came from Petunia's and the poor thing is just distraught! And Princess Sparkle Toes still hasn't seen one speck of fur from Mr. Cheeks. I thought you and your animals were doing something about this!"

I drew myself up to my full five feet and seven inches and straightened the Windsor knot on my tie. It was a nice burgundy silk today, and quite fetching, if I say so myself.

"Excuse me?" I glared at him until his blue eyes flicked away again. But they were back soon enough.

"You said you could find Sapphire," he began.

I held up a hand to stop him. "I did no such thing. I said I would try. And what are you doing to help? Besides glad handing with people over drinks!"

"Glad handing?" Yarrow asked, clearly confused. Young people didn't always understand my extra-antiquated slang, but I didn't have time to explain, so just waved a hand their way, signaling that I was brushing the question away.

Yarrow subsided, slumping against the counter like a

queer Gumby toy. Another reference they likely wouldn't understand.

"I was taking care of Petunia!" Sweetheart Digs hissed. His blue eyes turned icy. The self-proclaimed Mayor of Pride Street did not like being criticized. At all. He just swanned around the neighborhood, expecting everyone to applaud.

Speaking of swanning around. "What do you do for a living, anyway?"

That was another mystery I'd never figured out. And no one seemed to know, not even Bex and Jacki, and they knew everything about everyone in the neighborhood. Turns out when people were in that vulnerable, pre-caffeinated state, they said more than they should.

Which reminded me, I should check in with those two again. And maybe talk to Ace and Jerome, the two bartenders at Enrico's. What Bex and Jacki didn't hear, the two bartenders saw.

But that meant going to a nightclub. And being in a noisy crush of people. John would be thrilled, at least. Any excuse to don a pair of heels, and he was there. Maybe I could make him ask the questions while I hid behind a martini.

Sweetheart Digs stared at me, mouth working as if chewing something nasty. Yarrow and I both just stared at him in silence. Outside, a bicycle bell chimed.

Bicycle. Who did I know who rode bicycles? And was there a bike at old Charles's house? Or the house next door?

Maybe I'd take a walk later and investigate.

"I am in service to the community," Sweetheart Digs finally said, tilting up his face so his nose was in the air. What looked like diamond studs winked from his ears.

"Meaning you live off your trust fund, don't you?" Yarrow asked. "That's what people say, anyway. Is it true?"

Sweetheart's face flushed, and his lips pressed into a narrow line.

"New earrings?" I asked. "I don't think I've ever seen them before."

He touched the studs lightly.

"Yes," he sniffed. "Not that it's any of your business."

Then he turned on Yarrow. "And you. Just because you have no money doesn't mean the rest of us are bad for being rich!"

Then he spun on his heel and stomped out the door. He tried to slam it on its way out, but the pneumatic arm gave it a soft close as usual.

He shot daggers at us through the front window, then slapped those dark glasses back on his head, stalking away.

"Well, that hit a nerve," Yarrow remarked in a dry voice.

I smiled at them. "Sure did."

I stared out at the street, at the beautiful early summer day and the people walking by. And I wondered, why exactly had Sweetheart Digs come in?

What did he really want to find out?

I added that to my list of things to investigate. But first? I really needed to get back to work.

CHAPTER 18
Marsha

JOHN DECIDED he needed a break from writing "to walk and think."

I understand. I think best when I'm walking, too. But I didn't want to think too much today. Klaus and I needed to look around and sniff.

We headed down our street, scanning for gray cats, bicycles, and hamsters. Nothing but gardens and elm trees so far. We turned onto the section of Pride Street that had cherry trees. I dodged the fallen fruit. They hurt my paws. Klaus tried to eat one once, and almost choked on the hard pit.

That meant I also had to go to the vet because John and Garrett were both so worried about the dang fluff ball they both had to go, and Garrett insisted I come along "just in case," even though I wasn't the one with a pink stain around my mouth from cherry juice.

"Do you see that?" Klaus barked.

All I saw was Princess Sparkle Toes. She looked around, a huge pair of sunglasses covering half her face. It seemed like she saw us, but then she turned and stepped under a green striped awning, heading into the little grocery store where John sometimes bought a can of Coke. "Contraband," he called it. "Don't tell Garrett."

I didn't understand what he meant. Sure, I thought soda was disgusting, but humans ate and drank a lot of disgusting things. But I kept his secret, anyway.

"That was Sparkle Toes," I said. *"So?"*

"She had a pink plastic purse, just like the one Ron described!"

"The kind with breathing holes for her hamster?"

"Yes!"

I had been so sure Mr. Cheeks was dead… but what exactly had I smelled in his cage? And if he wasn't dead, why had Sparkle Toes said he was?

I pulled on my leash and broke into a run, causing John to shout in surprise. I didn't care. We had to get to the shop before Sparkle Toes left.

"What are you two doing?" John yelled. "Slow down!"

I didn't pause. I knew John could keep up. Unlike Garrett, John went running almost every day. That meant he could keep up with Klaus and me. It also meant his muscles were hard, so he was a little less comfy to sit on than Garrett, but that was okay. I loved John anyway.

I yelped as my front paw hit a cherry but kept going. I was determined to not let this clue get away.

Klaus and I barreled toward the green stripes of At Your Convenience, though the new ache in my paw slowed me down a bit. At least the cherry wasn't embedded between my foot pads. That was the worst.

We pulled to a stop, looking up at the heavy glass door and the windows that displayed what looked like dancing potato chips. The owner changed the windows every month, and they were always kind of weird. The humans liked them, though, so I guess they worked.

"You want to go into At Your Convenience? Why in the world? Tracy doesn't have dog treats."

I barked. *"Princess Sparkle Toes is inside!"*

John sighed. "Okay. Guess I'll get my weekly contraband a day early."

We backed off as he tugged on the heavy door, then entered the cool shop.

"Hi John!" Tracy said from the aisle to the right. A short, stocky woman with pale skin, ruddy cheeks, and short gray hair, Tracy wore a T-shirt that stretched over her square body, and loose jeans with a chain at the hip. I think it was attached to her wallet or something.

Garrett and John both said Tracy was an "old school butch," whatever that means. I just know she keeps dog treats on the front counter and is always nice to me and Klaus.

We trotted over for pets. Tracy had a box of cereal open at her boot-clad feet. The boots looked tastier than the cereal boxes, that was for sure.

"Hey you two!" She scratched Klaus and then me.

"They wanted to come in for some reason, so I figured I'd get a Coke," John said.

Right! Sparkle Toes! I sniffed the air for hamster, but it was hard to catch it. Tracy's store was filled with so. Many. Smells. Beer, soda, floor cleaner, chips, beef jerky, fancy olives—yuck—and my all-time favorite, cheese.

"Do you smell Mr. Cheeks?" I barked.

Klaus's little snoot was in the air. *"No. But I hear high heels."*

Sure enough, I caught the tell-tale clicking on the

linoleum floor. Sounded like it came from two aisles over. I tugged on my leash, pulling John along.

"Okay, okay!" he said. "I'm coming. Why the agenda today, Marsha?"

"*Sparkle Toes is here!*" Klaus barked in reply.

"You're ganging up on me," John muttered, but I could tell he wasn't actually upset.

We rounded the corner to the back aisle where the refrigerators hummed in a bright, white line. John paused. I tugged.

"Marsha P.! You wanted to come in here, but that means I need to get my Coke!"

I heard the heels clicking. Was Sparkle Toes getting away?

Pulling harder, I shot down the next aisle. Sure enough, there she was, rushing as fast as she could in her heels and purple pants, bare arms filled with snacks.

"*Sparkle Toes! Stop!*" I barked.

"*Stop! Stop! Stop!*" Klaus barked.

"What the heck?" John asked, but at least he followed us.

I put on a burst of speed and rammed into her long legs.

"Oof!" she exclaimed, snacks flying out of her arms. She stumbled but caught herself on a rack. I heard potato chips crunch under her hands.

"Are you okay?" Tracy asked, rushing to the aisle.

"Marsha P. Johnson!" John yelled. "What has gotten into you! You apologize to Princess Sparkle Toes. Right now!"

I was too busy sniffing to answer, staring up at her arm.

Klaus was right. Slung over the bangles on her wrist was a pink plastic purse with air holes in the top.

And staring back at me was a hamster, a cheese puff in his little paws. Bright round eyes blinked, then he shoved the entire cheese puff into his tiny mouth, causing his right cheek to bulge alarmingly.

Adam was right. Mr. Cheeks wasn't missing, and he wasn't dead, either.

And now I knew why he had that silly name.

"Sorry about the chips, Tracy!" Princess Sparkle Toes yanked open the front door.

"Stop! Stop!" I barked.

"Marsha P.! No barking indoors! How many times do we have to talk about that?"

I looked up at John to protest but saw that he was staring at the glass door, where, in a flash of purple pants, Princess Sparkle Toes disappeared.

CHAPTER 19

Garrett

I LOOKED up from my design mood board and stretched. It turned out that my client did want the emerald-green rather than sage, which was good news for me. I love saturated colors.

The shop door chimed, and in trotted Marsha and Klaus, followed by John. The corgis barked and pranced with excitement, and John looked slightly disheveled.

"What's going on?" I asked, rounding the counter. "I didn't expect a visit today!"

"We saw Sparkle Toes!" Marsha barked

"And Mr. Cheeks!" Klaus chimed in.

I looked at my partner. "What are they on about?"

He shook his head and bent to unhook their leashes. Both corgis zoomed down the central aisle, turned, and raced back again as we watched.

"I suspect they're trying to tell you we just saw Princess Sparkle Toes."

"And?"

"And she had that little purse Ron was talking about."

"The hamster habitat purse?"

John nodded.

Well. "And Mr. Cheeks was inside?"

John shrugged. "I couldn't tell, but this one seems to think so. She was barking her head off and chased Sparkle Toes out of Tracy's store."

Marsha barked again. I ignored her for a moment, narrowing my eyes at John. "You were getting a bonus Coke, weren't you? I thought we talked about that."

As fit as John is, he sometimes has trouble with his blood sugar levels and is supposed to limit his soda intake to one a week.

He held out his empty hands to show me the lack of a soda can, but I crossed my arms over my chest and glared.

"Look," he said, "can we not discuss this now? My sugar levels were fine last time."

Because he had stopped drinking three Cokes a day.

"You're the one who asked me to help keep you on track," I reminded him.

The bells chimed again, and Daniel rushed through the door, his usually golden skin looking pale, his sprinkling of pock marks standing out in high relief.

"Garrett! John! You have to come!"

"What?" My heart pounded in my chest.

"It's Petunia! She's dead!"

"What?" I shrieked, then grabbed my phone from the counter, donned the straw boater I'd left the house with, and helped John secure the corgis to their leashes again.

Then I paused. "Wait. If she's dead, where are we rushing off to? What happened?"

Daniel looked stricken. Tufts of his dark, silver-shot hair showed where he'd been tugging at it. He caught me looking and tried to smooth it with both hands.

"She's in the back of her shop. Will you come? See if Marsha and Klaus can sniff out anything?"

John and I shared a look. I could tell he didn't want me getting involved, but what can I do? It's my community and we were already involved, what with Sapphire and all the rest.

I looked back to Daniel, who was literally wringing his hands in distress.

"We'll come."

We all trooped out the door and hurried down the street to Flower Frenzy. The front of Petunia's shop looked mighty quiet.

"You didn't call the cops?" John asked.

Daniel held a set of keys up to the front door lock, but his hands shook so hard, he couldn't manage. I handed Marsha's leash to John and gently took the keys from Daniel's hands.

Soon enough, we were inside the shop. Water puddled on the checkerboard floor, gladiolas, gerbera daisies, and ferns were strewn about. Marsha and Klaus began sniffing.

"John! The dogs!" I said in alarm. "We have to make sure there's no glass!"

He yanked the leashes, hard, shortening the extensions and dragging both dogs toward him. Marsha yipped in protest.

As my eyes scanned the floor for shattered vases, I repeated John's question. "No cops?"

"No," Daniel replied. "I wanted to see if you could find anything first. And… Petunia didn't have the best relationship with the local police."

Not surprising. A lot of queer people don't. But I'd ask why Petunia didn't in particular later.

"Floor looks clear," John said.

"Okay." I turned to my partner. His mouth was set in an *I'm concerned and thinking about it* line. "If you stay here with the dogs, I'll go check on Petunia. Follow me in when you're ready?"

He nodded, already on it. I headed toward the back, followed by the hand-wringing Daniel. Were he and Petunia that close? Or was it just the thought of seeing her dead body again?

The back room was just as bright as before, but much less tidy. There wasn't the damage here there was out front, though some of the dried wreath supplies dangled from the wall, and a chair was overturned.

I saw a set of blue, chunky heels poking from behind the green table and walked slowly toward them, eyes scanning, careful to not step on anything that might be important. Though what exactly would prove to be important, I had no idea.

Bumped up against a table leg was a little silver ball. I fished my handkerchief from my pocket and bent to pick it up.

It was a stud earring. Wrapping it up, I pocketed the clue and continued toward Petunia.

The poor thing was splayed out in an undignified manner that would have mortified her if she'd been alive. Her arms were thrown back, her head turned to the side at a terrible angle, and a hairpiece dangled near her ear. Her makeup was smudged and, as I bent, I could see two of her fake fingernails had broken off.

She hadn't gone down without a fight.

Daniel hovered near the door. I couldn't blame him for not wanting to come closer, but I needed something.

"Daniel."

He looked at me, dark eyes wide with fright. I clapped my hands.

"Daniel! See if you can find a box of gloves!"

He nodded and began looking through some shelves.

"Who did this to you, Petunia?" I whispered. And then John was at my side, handing me a pair of blue nitrile gloves. I nodded thanks and slipped a pair on.

"Where are the dogs?" I asked.

"I tied them up in the other room. It looked like you need more time."

I did. I laid my fingers on Petunia's pale throat, just in case. No pulse. Running my fingers lightly over her skull, I found a big goose egg.

"What's that?" John asked, gesturing toward her chest.

Her chunky silver necklace dangled to one side of a big red mark, the impression of the large, central piece still lingering on her skin, as if something had pressed it, hard, against her.

"Looks like she was pushed."

I stood and scanned the room again, the objects around me telling the story of the fight.

"It looks like someone pushed her and she hit her head on the table, going down. And the impact angle did something to her neck."

Like snapping it, though I have no medical training, so couldn't really tell.

I looked at my thriller and mystery writer husband. "Could hitting her head kill her?"

John nodded. "If you hit something hard enough—or it hits you—that can cause a brain bleed. The blood builds pressure inside the skull. Either you go into a coma, or you die from lack of oxygen to the brain."

I shivered, glad for the knowledge, but disturbed all the same.

"So, it could have been an accident. But what a way to die," I said.

Daniel rushed from the room.

"I'll go after him," John said.

And then I was alone with a person I'd just been talking with the day before. A person whose cat may or may not be missing.

"Petunia, what in the world were you involved in? Who did this to you?"

But her dead body didn't seem to have anything else to say.

CHAPTER 20

Marsha

DANIEL RUSHED through the front of the shop. John came from the back room soon after but didn't say anything to us. Just glanced to make sure we were still tied up and headed outside.

I saw him talking to Daniel, who threw his hands into the air and burst into tears.

John pulled him in for a hug.

"Klaus!"

"What?"

"We have to get into the back room! Look for more clues!"

"But John told us we had to stay here! And besides," he tugged on his leash, *"he locked the extension thingie. We're stuck."*

Klaus was right, but I wasn't going to let that stop me. I gave one long pull. Nothing. Another. Still nothing.

"What are you doing?" Klaus complained. *"You're bumping me!"*

"So, scoot over a few inches. I'm trying to get this leash to extend!"

Klaus moved. I gave a sharp yank and felt something

click. One more sharp yank, and sure enough, the locking mechanism opened, unspooling the leash so fast I fell on my chin. Shaking my head at the indignity, I got back to my feet and began nosing my way toward the back.

We'd already sniffed around the front, but it was hard to catch any smells other than crushed flowers. I could smell what I thought was Petunia and a second person, but the trouble with shops is people are coming in and out all the time, making it hard for specific people smells to stand out.

But something about the second strongest scent made me pause. It smelled like human sweat, but kind of sour. I didn't like that smell at all.

"You're just leaving me?" Klaus whined.

"Tug hard. See if you can unlock. But one of us has to get into that back room before John gets back and stops us!"

I left my friend behind and sniffed my way toward the back. I didn't want to miss anything. Soon enough, I was heading down a little hallway, toward a light, bright room. I could hear Garrett moving around softly and walked as quietly as I could, hoping his movements would cover the click of my claws on the floor.

I also hoped my leash would extend far enough.

As soon as I cleared the hall, I saw the body splayed out on the other side of a tall table. She didn't look good. I sniffed my way toward her, then sniffed all the way around her body. Garrett hadn't seen me yet, which was good. Then my leash tugged me to a stop.

"Marsha P. Johnson." Garrett's voice sounded tired. "How in the world did you get back here?"

He held the middle of my leash in one hand and stared down at me, looking worried and sad. Then he sighed and let the leash drop.

"You may as well keep sniffing," he said. "You might have better luck finding something than I have."

I gave a soft bark and continued sniffing around Petunia. There was that sour smell again, but it wasn't Petunia. Petunia smelled… not good. My nose wrinkled. She smelled a bit like pee and her skin smelled off to me. Maybe that was just because she was dead.

But there was something just beneath her hip. Something shiny.

I pawed at it, trying to catch it with a claw. I pressed my nose into Petunia's hip, trying to clear some of the fabric from her dress out of my way. Ugh. Her dress really smelled like pee.

Then I pawed again and felt my front nails catch on something hard. I pulled it out.

"What do you have there?" Garrett crouched next to me, then reached out. He had on those weird blue gloves that smell kind of like Klaus's favorite rubber ball.

Holding the thing up to the light, we both looked at it. It was a small shard of brown glass. I pawed at Petunia's side some more.

"Marsha. Stop. Let me," Garrett said. He wrapped the glass in his handkerchief and carefully pressed against Petunia's side, looking for more glass. He brought out one more piece, a larger one.

"Sunglasses," he said. "Marsha P. Johnson, you found a broken sunglass lens. Good girl."

I panted happily at the praise but stopped when I heard John and Daniel's voices in the front of the store.

Even though I liked doing a good job, I wasn't here for the praise.

I was here because Petunia was dead, Sapphire was gone, and somebody was lying.

I looked up at Garrett, who pulled me away from the body.

"Let's go, girl," he said. "We need to call for someone to pick up Petunia."

I took one last look around but didn't see anything.

But as I followed my human toward the sound of John's voice, I felt uneasy.

Something was missing. And I didn't know what.

CHAPTER 21

Garrett

IT TOOK FOREVER to answer questions from the police. Daniel was still with them. John and I told him to text if he needed us. We wanted to stay, but the cops shooed us on our way after taking our statements.

I didn't bother mentioning the earring and shards of glass tucked in my pocket. The police hadn't wanted to hear about the missing cat or anything else. They were already attributing Petunia's death to a robbery gone wrong.

"This makes me sick," I said, shuffling along the sidewalk at John's side. Even Marsha and Klaus were subdued, walking obediently close to us, as if they'd been trained to heel.

Which they had, but that didn't usually work. Marsha was an instigator and Klaus followed her lead half the time, not ours.

John rubbed the back of my neck.

"You're getting a massage tonight," he said. "Your neck muscles feel ready to snap."

"Poor choice of words," I said.

"Oh! I'm sorry! I wasn't thinking."

I wanted to reply that he wasn't thinking because he killed people in his books all the time and didn't care. But I bit my tongue because, upset as I was, I knew that wasn't true. At all. John and I just showed we were upset in different ways. His was trying to take care of me.

My way? Was trying to take care of everyone else in the world.

I sighed and shuffled along. "I can't go back to work today, and I'm not ready to go home."

There was no way I could work on projects or help customers. And no way would I relax if we went home.

"Want to stop at Bruiser's? Or at Ron's?"

I paused on the sidewalk, letting people pass us by. Everyone looked so happy to be out in the sunshine, flirting or taking a break from work. Didn't they know Petunia was dead?

"Let's stop by Bruiser's, I guess. I could use an iced green tea." My stomach growled, telling me we'd long since missed lunch. I felt incredulous that I was hungry, but my stomach doesn't lie.

"Sounds like you should eat something, too."

"You can take the time off work?"

John shrugged. "I'll make up my words tomorrow."

He would, too. My sweetheart had the discipline and dedication of a triathlete when it came to his writing. He always said that a combination of discipline and luck were the keys to his success.

"Text Ron and see if he can meet us?" I asked.

Once it became clear we were heading to Bruiser's Best Beans, Klaus and Marsha picked up the pace. I was sure they wanted to share the news with Bruiser. Once again, I wished the dogs could talk.

We walked into Bruiser's with the dogs. As my eyes adjusted to the interior, I saw that Bex and Jacki must have already heard the news. Jacki's eyes were damp, as if she'd been crying, and Bex looked ready to punch something.

We all deal with grief and shock our own ways.

"Hey," I said. "Looks like you heard."

Bex nodded. "You were there?"

I nodded back. Jacki pressed her hands to her eyes, then inhaled and straightened up, adjusting the bright green patterned head scarf that ringed her head, framing her short cap of dark curls.

"I just can't believe it," she said. "What happened?"

I looked around. No one was in line behind us, and the few people in the café had earbuds in and laptops open. It was the after-lunch lull.

"It looks as if she was attacked. There were signs of a struggle."

"Who do you think did it?" Bex asked, eyes sharp.

I played with one of the buttons on my shirt and looked at John.

"Up to you," he said.

I leaned across the counter and lowered my voice. "I found a silver stud earring and Marsha found some broken sunglass lenses."

"Those could belong to anyone. I mean, how many people in this neighborhood wear sunglasses and earrings?" Bex asked.

Bex was right. The answer was just about everyone.

"Look," I said, "the cops think it's just a robbery gone wrong, so…"

Bex slapped a hand on the counter hard enough that Marsha barked and two people looked up from their laptops.

She flashed a fake smile around. We all waited until everyone went back to work.

"No way," she hissed. "With Sapphire missing, and Mr. Cheeks, and all the rest of it? No way this was a robbery!"

John cleared his throat. "Actually, I think Mr. Cheeks is still alive."

Both women looked at him, jaws dropped.

"What?" Jacki asked.

"Sparkle Toes had her little hamster purse this morning. And she ran away when Marsha P. tried to get close."

"Sparkle Toes wears sunglasses," Bex said. "But I think she usually wears dangly earrings."

"No!" Jacki said. "I mean, yes. She does. But doesn't Princess Sparkle Toes also have a stud piercing higher up her ear?"

"I don't remember," I said. At the same time John said, "She does."

I looked at him and he shrugged.

"I'm a writer. Details are important."

Okay.

"And Vyviane was in here the other day, looking for an earring. And she wears sunglasses."

My head started to throb, then my stomach growled. And it was loud this time.

"I hate to do this to you," I said. "But can we continue this discussion while I eat? I missed lunch."

"Sure," Jacki said. "Spinach with chicken pesto panini sound good?"

My stomach growled again. "Sounds great. And an iced green tea, please."

John ordered the same, and we took the dogs to a table near the back, away from the scattered patrons who mostly populated the prime window seats. Once the dogs were settled with a savory cookie each, John got out his phone and opened a notes app.

"So. Who do we have, so far?" he asked, and started typing with his thumbs. "Sparkle Toes, for one. And?"

I thought back to everyone I'd seen wearing sunglasses, which, given that it was summer, was quite the list.

"Sweetheart Digs always wears his fancy sunglasses. And I noticed he had new earrings, too."

John tapped away.

"Vyviane was wearing sunglasses when we saw her at the Sapphire search party. And she has a row of studs up one ear."

I felt slightly guilty naming my ex. Just because she is a terrible person who trampled my heart doesn't mean she's a murderer. Cat thief, maybe. But could she kill?

If the murder really was accidental, maybe. I could see Vyviane fighting someone if the stakes were high enough.

Bex brought our tea in giant, ice-filled pint glasses. "Be right back with your food."

I traced a finger through the condensation on my glass, staring into the pale green brew as if it could answer any of the questions crashing in my head. I took a deep breath, trying to calm my nervous system after the events of the day.

"It's summer," I continued, "so I don't really think the sunglass lenses are that helpful in narrowing anyone down. It could be almost anyone, John. But what I don't get is, what's up with the missing animals, and the lies? Is it more blackmail, do you think?"

The last terrible death in our little village-in-the-city was because a waiter at Daniel's restaurant was black-mailing people.

He tapped a finger against his lips. His dark eyes scanned the street in front of the café, but I could tell he wasn't really seeing anything. He was coming up with possible plot points and connections. That was how his writer brain worked.

And people think my brain is weird. Try living with a novelist.

Bex and Jacki returned with our food and their own lunches.

"I may need to jump up," Bex said, "but this one hasn't eaten all day."

She jerked a thumb at her partner. Jacki's mouth was already full of delicious smelling panini. I followed suit.

Yep. Chicken pesto with spinach? Delicious.

We all ate for a minute or two, but I could feel Bex's leg jouncing with impatience.

I took another bite, hoping to buy more thinking time, but she couldn't wait any longer.

"I hope you're not taking the cop's word on this, Garrett. We have to take care of our own."

"Babe," Jacki said in warning.

"No! Garrett, you have to investigate."

"Why me?" I asked.

"Because you're the only one people around here trust. And besides, you figured out who killed Saschi, didn't you?"

Well, sort of. I figured out who wanted Saschi dead but… it's complicated.

Marsha P. barked and got to her feet, saving me from answering.

But when I looked up to see what she was barking at?

It was Roderick Gauge. The man who had wanted Saschi dead.

And he had dark glasses on. A different pair than he'd been wearing last time I saw him peering through the window at Bones, Dogs, and Harmony.

CHAPTER 22

Marsha

THAT MAN RODERICK stormed into the café and stomped over to our table. I was on my feet, growling.

"Marsha!" John said, his voice sharp. "I'm sorry, Roderick. I don't know what's come over her today."

Roderick ignored both of us, whipping off his sunglasses and replacing them with clear glasses, like the kind Garrett wears.

Garrett studied him for a moment. "I thought you had transition lenses. The kind that go from regular to dark."

Roderick waved a hand like he was batting away a fly. I do that with my tail sometimes, and feel sorry for Bruiser, who has no tail and just has to suffer.

"Lost them. And that's not what I'm here to talk about."

I barked again. I really didn't like the way he was talking to Garrett. John reached down to soothe me. But I noticed he didn't tell me to be quiet.

"Klaus," I woofed softly, *"if he does anything, you take his left ankle, and I'll take his right."*

"Gotcha," Klaus woofed back. He stood up, ready to bite at a moment's notice.

"You've ruined my business!" Roderick fumed.

"What?" Garrett asked. I could hear the confusion in his voice. "Roderick, frankly, I don't even know what your business is!"

"Oh. You do. Your dogs are both wearing my things!"

I was?

"We are?" Klaus woofed.

John stood up. Klaus and I flanked him. "Roderick, no one here knows what you're talking about. And I don't appreciate you storming in here and threatening my husband while we're eating lunch with our friends."

Roderick trembled with anger. I stood poised to wrap my jaws around his ankle if I needed to. I mean, I don't usually bite anyone, but when John or Garrett are threatened? Watch out. Corgis can be fiercer than you think.

"I don't see how you can say that," Roderick replied. It sounded like he was shoving the words out through his teeth. Humans are so expressive with all the different sounds they make.

"Roderick," Jacki said, voice gentle. "I really don't think Garrett knows what you're talking about."

"You make dog and cat clothing and accessories, right?" Bex chimed in.

Oh! Roderick must have made the plaid collar I had on today. It's one of my favorites. Really shows up against my fur. At least, that's what Klaus told me.

"That's you?" Garrett asked. "You're Animal Antics? I love your stuff!"

"Then why did you tell Ron you were interested in Sophie Stuart's line of accessories? He cut my order by a third in order to get some in."

Uh oh. That didn't sound good.

"Roderick, I truly had no idea. I'm sorry. Can I buy you a coffee? Kombucha? Tea? Heck, I'll buy you a sandwich if you want one."

Roderick's arms were crossed over his chest, but he relented.

"Okay. Iced coffee, please. With coconut milk."

Bex started to stand, but Jacki pushed back from the table. "I'll get it."

All the humans rearranged themselves at the table.

"Can I sit back down, now?" Klaus asked.

"I guess we may as well."

We settled ourselves next to Bruiser, who had remained alert this whole time but hadn't gotten up.

"So, what are you all talking about?" Roderick asked.

The whole table was silent.

Awkward.

Jacki came back with Roderick's coffee. I could smell it. It didn't smell nearly as good as the sandwiches, though. And I was a little miffed at Roderick for interrupting when he did. John and Garrett completely forgot to give us a bite.

Garrett cleared his throat, the way humans do when they don't want to say something.

"Petunia is dead."

I heard choking noises. Then coughing. I looked up. Roderick held his fist over his mouth, and his face was turning red.

"You okay, man?" John sounded concerned.

Roderick nodded and held up his other hand, one finger pointing to the ceiling.

"Oh my gosh," he said. Then he shoved his chair back. "Excuse me. I think I'm going to be sick."

He ran to the back of the café, past the counter.

"That was strange," Klaus woofed. *"Was Roderick close to Petunia?"*

"I don't know," I barked back. *"But you never know how humans will respond to death."*

Bruiser sighed, then farted. Gross.

"I think Roderick killed Petunia," the bulldog said.

"What?" I yipped.

"When Bex and I were in the flower store the other day, I heard them arguing before we opened the door. Roderick didn't seem happy."

"What were they saying?" I asked.

The bulldog looked mournful. But he kind of always looks that way.

"I couldn't hear. But after we came in, Roderick didn't stay."

"We have to tell Garrett and John!" I leapt up and started barking.

"Marsha P.!" John said. "We're trying to have an important conversation here!"

"And you know what the rules are about using your indoor voice." Garrett reached out and ruffled the fur on my head. I ducked from under his hand. This was no time for head pats.

"That's what I'm trying to tell you about! Bruiser heard something important!"

"Yes!" Klaus backed me up. *"You have to listen to Bruiser."*

"It's okay. I'm used to not being listened to." Bruiser's voice was gravelly and low. He sounded a little dejected.

"You too, huh Bruiser?" Jacki peered at the bulldog. "I really think they're all trying to tell us something."

"Yeah, but what?" Bex asked.

I was about to open my mouth to explain when Roderick stumbled up to the table. He looked terrible.

"Sorry. That was just a shock. I, uh, think I need to go."

He wove through the café. We all watched as he looked one way, then the other, before crossing the street and stalking away.

"What the heck was that about?" Bex asked. "You don't think he knows something, do you?"

I watched Garrett carefully. He had his thoughtful look on, and his eyes narrowed behind his glasses.

"I think it's more than a little odd that Roderick's sunglasses are different, for one thing."

"Yeah," Bex said. "But he almost puked when he found out Petunia was dead. That means he couldn't have anything to do with it. Right?"

No one said anything.

"Right?" Bex repeated.

Everyone stared down at their coffee drinks. I slumped back down to the floor, really wishing I had something to chew on.

Chewing helps me think. And right now?

I had a lot of thoughts to sort out inside my head.

CHAPTER 23

Adam

JOHN AND GARRETT were fixing dinner in the kitchen. I loved watching their dance. Refrigerator to sink to stove to chopping board, they moved around each other as if they'd done the moves a thousand times.

And they had.

And that was a thing that gave me a pang where my heart used to beat. I missed that sort of easy intimacy. The quiet moments, when all two people had to do was enjoy each other's company as they went about the tasks that make up the rhythm of life.

"I really wish I didn't have to deal with this," Garrett complained. "It's too much. And that thing with Roderick? I just don't know what to think."

The small, slightly chubby man pushed his tortoise-shell glasses higher on the bridge of his nose and resumed slicing up zucchini as John heated oil in a big pan. The zucchini came from the garden out back, I knew. Marsha was convinced she could get me out there someday, but so far I'd been too chicken to try.

I mean, sure, I had assumed I wasn't able to leave the building because of some supernatural ghost rules, but really? I was afraid. What if I stepped outside the walls of the house and disappeared? Could I get back inside somehow? Or would I just be gone? Forever.

"You're already involved, babe. The question is, what are you going to do about it?"

"Do about it?" Garrett's voice rose. "Examining Petunia's dead body wasn't enough?"

John turned the heat down on the pan and moved behind Garrett, wrapping his long, honey-colored arms around the much smaller, paler man. I watched as some of the tension left Garrett's body. He sighed and leaned his seal brown hair against John's navy T-shirt.

"I hate this," Garrett said.

"I know, babe. I know. But I'm here to help."

"*So are we!*" Marsha barked.

That, at least, got Garrett to smile.

"Okay. These are ready for the pan. And the lamb chops smell good."

"That they do."

John returned to the stove and sautéed the vegetables.

I wished I could smell better. What I have is more like the memory of a smell. I could almost remember what lamb chops cooking smelled like, though we didn't have them often. We never had money for food like that, relying on beans, rice, spaghetti and the like. Zucchini though? We ate those all summer long.

"What's your plan?" John asked, leaning against the counter. I wanted to know the same thing.

The dogs were strangely silent. They'd eaten their dinners and gone to lie down in the living room.

When I'd asked Marsha about it, she'd mentioned the dead florist and that it had been a very tiring day. I wasn't sure what to think about it and told her to follow the money.

After all, even watching my best friends die? Had ended up being about money. Greed, money, and fear.

"What did you think about Roderick?" John asked.

Garrett just shrugged. The poor guy looked defeated.

"I don't know what to think about this whole situation. Sparkle Toes. The missing cat. Petunia dead. Roderick acting weird… and there's something going on with Sweetheart Digs, too."

Garrett removed his glasses and pinched the bridge of his nose.

"I just wish I could figure out how it's all connected."

::*Follow the money*,:: I whispered in his ear. He scratched his ear, which told me at least he felt something.

What else could I do? Ah. His wallet. He'd set his phone, wallet, and keys on the counter near the door between the kitchen and dining room. How far could I move it? Could I move it at all?

I'd been practicing with small objects, but so far my biggest success had been with moving paper. Garrett turned to the sink and began washing cutting boards and knives. John took a cast iron pan from the oven. The lamb chops.

"These just need to rest for a minute or two. And the zucchini is done."

I walked to the pile of Garrett's stuff and reached, my hand going through the keys. I planted my big boots on the floor, braced myself, and used every ounce of my will to push the slim leather wallet.

"Thanks, babe. I appreciate you cooking all the time."

"You know I enjoy it. It helps to make something nice after blowing things up or killing people all day."

I looked up at that to see John wince.

"Sorry," he said. "That was a little insensitive."

Garrett turned, wiping his hands on a dish towel. He gave John a soft smile that melted me to my ghostly toes. "That's okay. It's not as if I don't know what you do for a living."

The wallet hadn't budged. Try, try, again.

Nothing. Gah. Then I had a thought.

::Hey, Marsha!:: I called out.

A couple of seconds later, I heard claws on the dining room floor. Then the little black corgi was at my boots, waving that frond of a tail.

"Yes?"

::Can you get this wallet for me?::

"And do what?"

::I don't know. Drag it to the floor? We have to find a way to convince John and Garrett to follow the money.::

Klaus came in and yawned. *"What's going on?"*

"I'm going to knock Garrett's wallet to the floor, and you're going to run with it into the living room."

"Won't we get in trouble?"

Marsha narrowed her eyes at Klaus, looking so much like an old queen admonishing a younger performer that I almost laughed.

::We are doing this for the good of the case, Klaus,:: I replied.

"Who knew Roderick made dog and cat clothes and stuff?" Garrett asked.

"Well, clearly someone knew. And I guess he had to do something after he couldn't really work for the bank anymore. But I don't see what that has to do with Petunia's death. Or any of the rest of it."

"Sapphire missing is still bothering me," Garrett said, as John began to plate their food.

"Follow the money!" Marsha barked. Then she put her paws up on the counter. She barely reached. I tried to help and managed to shove the wallet half an inch toward her waiting mouth. She grabbed a corner, dragged it to the floor, then barked, *"Run, Klaus! Run!"*

Klaus, the little trooper, grabbed the wallet in his mouth like it was a rat and scrambled off, chased by Garrett. We all headed to the living room, where Klaus danced and pranced, back and forth, as Garrett chased him around the coffee table.

"What has gotten into you two?" he shouted. "John! Help!"

John swooped in with his longer arms and grabbed Klaus from across the coffee table.

"Drop!" he commanded.

Klaus opened his jaws obediently, and the slim wallet fell to the coffee table, the corner of a twenty-dollar bill peeking out.

That, I could work with. I leaned over and tugged at the bill, sending it floating in the air.

"Did you see that?" Garrett whispered.

"Unreal," John replied, still clutching a kicking Klaus. "Do you think that was Adam?"

Both men looked at each other. I willed them to please understand.

"Yes! It's Adam! Pay attention!" Marsha barked.

::Thanks, Marsha. You too, Klaus.::

Klaus wriggled to get down, and John set him on the floor. But Garrett was looking right at me. Or, right past me. But at least his eyes were trained toward where I stood.

"You think this is about money, don't you, Adam?" he said, understanding dawning in his eyes.

Finally. Yes. They understood.

I just hoped it helped.

CHAPTER 24
Garrett

PERCHED on my high stool behind the front counter, I traced the silver band on my right pointer finger. After last night's stunt with the wallet and the twenty-dollar bill, I decided I may as well try keeping something of Adam's on me. It seemed pretty clear he wanted to communicate with us and was trying more and more.

Whether the ring would strengthen the connection or not, only time would tell. The wide band had likely been Adam's pinkie ring. He was a much larger person than I am, but it felt good on my center finger.

Unlike being at work. Usually I enjoyed my work, but this day? Being in the shop felt like torture, but I had clients to satisfy, and that meant I needed to finalize designs. Next Monday when the shop was closed, I really needed to be at the homes of my two current clients, supervising painters in one and moving in furniture on the second. That meant I had to double check all my orders and make sure the painters had the correct colors so they could get an early start.

I put my fancy "back in fifteen minutes" sign on the front door, locked it, then headed to the back room to make a cup of tea.

I really needed to think about hiring someone to take care of the store so I could take on more clients. Clients paid better than walk-in furniture sales, and I needed the business. It was a classic you need to spend money to make money move, but one that made me nervous, all the same.

The shop was slow, as it usually is on weekdays, but that didn't mean I could just shut down to go on client calls. In order for a store to be successful, it needed continuity. But that was a problem for another day.

"Spend money to make money," I muttered, as I poured steaming water from the electric kettle into the waiting blue ceramic mug. I preferred classic floral teacups, but finally admitted they just weren't big enough if I wasn't making an entire pot, so John had gotten me this beauty.

Adam had said to follow the money. Or at least, I assume that was what the whole wallet trick was about. Pretty slick, enlisting the corgis to help him out like that.

On the surface, follow the money made sense, but when I looked at all the moving parts? It still didn't add up. Pun intended.

Tea in hand, I walked the store, making slight adjustments to some of the displays. In a moment, I'd get out pen and paper, but right now, I needed movement to help me think.

Sipping my tea, I headed to the Craftsman furniture section and plopped on the comfy burnt orange upholstery of one of the classic wood armchairs. I could see the door from here and still feel tucked away, rather than on display, like in the Deco section closer to the front.

Then I pulled out my phone and opened a notes app. Pen and paper would be better, but I didn't feel like sitting behind the counter anymore. Or getting out of this chair.

The week's events had taken a lot out of me, which is why I left the dogs at home today. One less thing to keep track of.

Money? I tapped out, following the word by a blank spot.

Motive? And then, finally, the most important thing, and the part of the list I always hated making.

Suspects.

A knock came at the front door. It was Vyviane. With her cloud of blonde hair and her trim, tiny figure. She took the sunglasses off her face and cupped a hand on the glass to cut down the glare.

Great. I'd have to polish her hand print off the door.

I sat very still, hoping she wouldn't see me and just be on her way. But nope. Those blue eyes scanned the store and landed right on me. Her face lit in a smile worthy of Sweetheart Digs, and she motioned for me to unlock the door.

Busted.

Groaning, I headed toward the front, dropping my mug on the counter as I went, then unlocked the front door. But instead of ushering my ex inside, I braced myself in the door jamb.

"Hello Vyviane. What can I do for you?"

She pouted her glossy peach painted lips. "Come on, Garrett. Aren't you going to let me in? I need to talk to you."

Her eyes flicked sideways on that last sentence, as if someone was listening.

Or as if she was looking for someone.

I sighed and opened the door. "Come in."

Sometimes, going up against the woman took more energy than just giving Vyviane her way. Which was probably why she was such a successful grifter.

I took the sign off the door. May as well be open for business. And maybe a customer would save me from this conversation.

Vyviane waltzed directly to the Deco section, the chunky heels of her sandals clomping on the floor, pale legs flashing beneath her short white denim skirt, until she reached the big carpet I half hoped would sell and half hoped wouldn't. It was a beauty, woven in shades of burgundy, green, and gold, and was worth a lot. I could use the cash, but it framed this section perfectly, making me loath to part with it.

She sat on the blue velvet sofa with a flounce of ruffled white shirt, setting her minuscule handbag next to her.

I followed but perched on the arm of one of the over-stuffed Deco chairs, not willing to give her more time than necessary.

There was that pout again.

"Come on, Garrett. Just sit down. It's not as if I'll bite you or anything."

No. You'll just insult me, undermine my self-confidence, and stomp on my heart as you leave.

"Although, I seem to recall you kind of liked it when I bit," she simpered coyly.

Queasiness and anger roiled in my gut. I gripped my hands together and fought to slow my breathing down. The last thing I needed was an emotional meltdown. Especially in front of her. That would just give Vyviane more ammunition for whatever grift she was plotting now.

Follow the money. Vyviane was always doing that, not to solve a mystery, but in order to get her talons on it.

"Stop it," I said. "Tell me what you want. Clock's ticking. I have work to do."

Her head snapped back as if I'd struck her, and a flash of anger crossed her eyes, then was gone, but her fake, sunny expression was harder now. Vyviane hated it when people called her bluff.

I was proud of myself. Old me would have never dared say anything like that to Vyviane.

"I'm not sure why you hate me, Garrett. What did I ever do to you? People break up all the time."

I sighed. "I don't hate you. I just don't like you very much. You're mean, Vyviane. And you use people. Now, are you going to tell me why you're here, or keep dancing around it?"

I looked at my watch, then back to her. Message sent.

"I wanted to know if you had any leads. About Petunia. Everyone is really upset about it, especially Sweetheart Digs. Daniel, too."

"You've been hanging around Sweetheart a lot, haven't you?" I asked.

She shrugged her narrow shoulders. "So? He's where it's at."

Vyviane looked around my store, as if passing judgement. "Maybe if you hung out with him more, you'd have more business."

I just stared at her, not rising to the bait. What had happened to old Garrett, who would have been squirming by now? Years of being with a man who treated me well, I guess. And having friends who actually like and respect me. But I didn't need to tell Vyviane any of that. The last thing I needed was for her to glom onto my friends.

She deflated slightly.

"I wanted to know if you saw anything unusual at Petunia's store. And whether you'd found Sapphire yet."

My eyes narrowed. What exactly was she fishing for. "You mean, besides Petunia's body? That was pretty unusual. And why do you care about Sapphire?"

"What?" she asked. "I can't care about a cat? What kind of monster do you think I am?"

She stood abruptly and grabbed her tiny purse. "I don't have to stay here and be insulted. I was only trying to help you on your case. Like, I figured we could share information, or something."

I stood myself and faced off with her. She was an inch taller than me in those chunky heels and tried to look down her nose at me. But I was done with that. I drew myself up to my full height.

"What information do you have, Vyviane?"

She smiled then, a cold and wicked smile.

"Too late, Garrett. You had your chance."

Then she turned and clomped out of my store. The bells chimed their friendly chime. She tried to slam the door, but the pneumatic struts wouldn't let her.

Score another one for me.

I pulled my phone back out of my pocket and thumbed in a message for John.

Vyviane just here, asking questions.

Three dots floated in response, finally forming into words.

You okay? Need me to come over?

My heart filled with love.

Nah. I'm good. But come by when you're done. We need to talk to Ron.

His thumbs-up emoji came as I walked to the counter, grabbed a notepad, and uncapped my favorite rollerball pen.

Time to get to the suspect list. And Vyviane's name was definitely on it now.

CHAPTER 25
Marsha

JOHN SAID we were going to get Garrett for dinner and then go to Ron's house, and Klaus was beside himself with joy.

"Can we invite Bruiser, too?" he woofed.

"Humans don't let us invite anyone. You know that." But I really wished they would. *"But maybe we can go by the café on our way and give John the idea."*

Humans were easy to control if you had the skill. I learned to vary my tactics, though. When a dog repeats things too many times, humans wise up. That's where most dogs go wrong.

John took a side route.

"You two need some exercise," he said as we trotted along. Luckily, this was a street with elm trees and maples. Not a cherry stone in sight on the well-swept sidewalks.

"We're going to see the man!" Klaus barked.

He was right.

"Eyes peeled for Sapphire," I reminded him. That search seemed to have stalled out, and it concerned me. I mean, I understand that a dead human meant more to John and

Garrett than a missing show cat, but she was where this whole mess began.

I just had to find a way to remind them.

We were almost at the house with the purple door. I sniffed all around, slowing John down. He sighed but paused all the same.

"*Smell anything?*" Klaus asked.

"*Not yet.*"

I headed to the fence post where Garrett found what we thought was Sapphire's fur. Nothing.

I snuffled along to the flower beds at old Charles's house. If I wanted to hide, his wild garden would be just the place.

"What a pretty garden," John said. "I can see why you two like it."

Two bicycles went by, ringing their bells, the people on them laughing. I wondered about the bicycle Ron saw. The one with the cat carrier. Had that really been Sapphire? And had she really escaped?

Or was she somewhere else? Maybe Charles would know.

I tugged my leash, hoping it would miraculously extend itself without too much effort. Nope. John must have had his thumb on the release button. Drat. I headed as far up the walkway as I could before he tugged me back.

"Marsha P.! Where do you think you're going?"

The purple door opened, and Charles's smiling brown face with its cap of short silver curls appeared.

"*Charles!*" I barked.

"Well, well, well. Look who came to visit! Hello there, Marsha P. Johnson and Klaus Nomi."

I felt John release our leashes and barked happily. Tails

wagging, we headed up the walk and onto the small wood porch.

Charles sat on the porch chair and reached out his hands. I shoved my head under one, and Klaus, under the other. Charles knew just where to scratch. Bliss.

"I see you've met my dogs," John said.

"Oh, yes. Another nice young man came by with them last week. Your partner, I assume? He was looking for a cat."

"That would be Garrett, all right. I'm John. Beautiful old Victorian you have here. Don't see many of these one-story cottages around."

"Yes. Well. I'm very fond of it. I love to take care of old things," he said, but didn't stop scratching behind my ears. I wiggled my butt with pleasure. "Pleased to meet you, John. I'm Charles. And I'm glad you came by today."

"Oh?" John asked.

"After your partner left, my nephew saw a fluffy gray cat in our backyard. Managed to coax her to the back porch with some food and water, but she wouldn't come in. Skittish, that one. Ran when Xavier tried to grab her. But we didn't know how to get ahold of you."

"Really? Do you know where she is now?"

Charles's face lit up with a smile. "Sure do. I sent Xavier to that pet shop with the silly name to get a cat bed. She's on the back porch now, taking a snooze."

"Mind if we…?"

"Pathway's right there, between the hydrangeas. Head on back. I'll tell Xavier not to sound the alarm."

"Did you hear that?" I barked excitedly, then tugged my leash, heading between the flowers and bushes, following the path around the house, Klaus panting at my heels.

When we rounded the corner, I saw another garden, this one with a tiny patch of grass surrounded by more flower and vegetable beds, like the kind we had at our house. Some furniture was set up on a broad wood deck, and, eyes slitted open, staring at us from a green bed, was Sapphire.

Her luxuriant gray fur was a bit tangled and matted, but she looked okay.

"*Sapphire!*" Klaus barked, pulling John toward the deck.

She stood and arched her back, hissing.

"Sapphire?" John's voice was gentle. "Everyone has been looking for you."

Once she figured out he wasn't going to grab her, she settled back onto her bed.

"*Sapphire, what happened?*" I barked.

"*A mean person yelled at Petunia and stole me. They stuffed me in a crate! And put me on a bicycle! I have never been treated so badly in my entire life!*"

"Whoa," Klaus said.

The back door opened, and there stood Charles and his nephew. The young man looked worried.

"Are you here to take the cat? I've been trying to take care of her, but she's kind of mean." We all looked at Sapphire, who gave a small meow. "Or maybe she's just scared and upset."

I gave her a friendly bark.

"*I didn't know who to trust!*" she yowled. "*And I was living off dog kibble and chicken sandwich crusts until he got me some real food!*"

Kibble and chicken sandwich crusts sounded good to me, but Sapphire didn't seem so happy about it.

John crouched down on the deck and held out a hand.

"Hey there, Sapphire. You remember me? I visited Petunia and petted you."

Sapphire was very still. I could tell she was weighing her options.

"You could come home with us," Klaus barked. *"John and Garrett will keep you safe."*

She looked shocked. *"But then I'd have to live with dogs! And who will brush my silver fur? And take me to my competitions?"*

Sapphire really was snooty. She'd probably try to lord it over me and Klaus in our own home. I started to turn away.

"Marsha!" Klaus yipped. *"We have to help her."*

I sighed and turned back to the gray, er silver cat. Her matted fur was pretty pitiful, and Xavier was right. She did look scared.

"It's us or the streets, Sapphire. Or back to the cat thieves," I said. *"There's plenty of room in the house for you."*

"And I won't have to eat chicken sandwich crusts?" she sniffed.

"No way!" Klaus barked. *"Those are all for Marsha and me!"*

"Are they… having a conversation?" Xavier asked. "It sure sounds like it."

John and Charles both laughed.

"You didn't grow up around animals," Charles said. "They're always discussing their own business, just like the folks in this neighborhood."

"That's the truth," John said. Then he looked back at Sapphire. "What do you think, Sapphire? I can take you to Leo's Grooming Palace and get you cleaned up. And I'm sure Ron has some nice things we can set up for you at our place."

Then Sapphire looked at us.

"Wait. Is it still not safe for me back at Petunia's? Then why would it be safe at Garrett and John's?" She blinked at me.

I squirmed a little.

"I'm sorry!" Klaus barked, then backed away.

"Sorry for what?" Sapphire hissed. *"What are you not telling me?"*

*"Petunia is dead, Sapphire. Daniel and Garrett found her."*I said.

Sapphire was completely still for a moment, then let out a piteous yowl.

"What's wrong with her?" Xavier asked. "She yowled like that when I found her but seemed to calm down when I got her some food."

"I don't know cats," John replied. "But she sounds sad to me. Maybe somewhere in her heart, she knows Petunia isn't coming back."

I nosed my way closer to Sapphire's bed, and she actually let me. That's how upset she was.

"Sapphire? I think John and Garrett are your best bet. Unless you want to stay here with Xavier and Charles."

She looked up at the older man and his nephew, then at me, Klaus, and John. Sapphire took in a shuddering breath, rose from her bed, and walked with mincing steps toward Xavier. She bumped his shin with her head, then turned and bumped Charles, too.

"What do you think, John?" I barked at my own human.

John smiled. "Charles and Xavier, looks like you have yourself a cat if you're willing to take her."

Charles looked fit to bust, he was so pleased. "I could use a companion for when this one here is at school."

He turned to his nephew. "What do you think, son?"

Xavier nodded. "Sounds good to me."

He bent carefully and held his hands out to Sapphire, gesturing that he wanted to pick her up. He didn't grab her, which was probably smart. The matted silver-gray cat actually nestled in his arms and let him stand with her!

Xavier wrinkled his nose. "But I think you're right about the grooming place. This one needs a bath."

Sapphire wasn't purring yet, but I could tell she was going to be okay.

Then John's face darkened. "But you'll need to keep her inside. And for now? I wouldn't spread it around much that she's here."

"Why not?" Xavier asked, confused.

"Because we think Sapphire's human was murdered."

Charles's face hardened. "I may be old. But that doesn't mean I'm defenseless."

Next to him, Xavier straightened his shoulders, which couldn't have been easy, considering Sapphire now clung to him like moss on a tree.

"No one is getting this cat," he said.

"Good," John replied. "Now, do you have anything you can hide her in? I'll call Leo and tell him we need to use the VIP back entrance."

"You can all take my car," Charles replied, then leaned toward Sapphire. She sniffed his nose. "No one is going to hurt a hair on this precious baby's head."

Sounded like Sapphire found a home. Now we just had to figure out who killed Petunia.

CHAPTER 26

Garrett

I **WAS STILL** in the shop, pretending to work, but other than helping a couple of customers, I'd been staring at my notepad or off into space.

John had called and told me about Sapphire and that he was taking the dogs to Leo's to drop her off. Then the plan was to head to Ron's for supplies.

Turns out Charles and Xavier not only found her, but would take her in. Good news. John suggested I meet them at Ron's store, and I might just.

But first? I had research to do. And more questions to ask.

I also had to admit that Vyviane's visit had thrown me off. She didn't have a hold over me anymore, which felt good. But now that I had cleared the miasma of self-doubt and hurt? Who she was shone clear as a summer dawn.

I'd known she was a manipulative grifter, and greedy, too. But today? I saw just how nasty a piece of work she really was. I used to just think she was using her dubious skills as a way to survive, and maybe to fill a hole of need inside. We all have those, don't we? And maybe those things were still true of Vyviane, too.

But mostly? I think she uses people because she enjoys it. And for the first time I realized she'd do anything to get what she wants. And that could include kidnapping and murder.

It shook me, to think I could have dated someone like that. And I wasn't ready to talk with John about it yet. Maybe after all this was over, I would. And he could tell me about his past with Sweetheart Digs. Right now, though, we had a murder to solve. Sapphire might be back, but she was likely still in danger. And there was no avoiding the fact that Petunia was stone cold dead.

I looked down at the list I'd made earlier. My suspect list disturbed me. I hate thinking poorly of people in my community, especially when we all needed to have each other's backs. But now that one of us was dead? I had no choice.

The names swam up from the white paper, inky black marks that chilled me to the bone.

Princess Sparkle Toes.

Sweetheart Digs.

Roderick, who was on the list last time. And I wasn't sure if that made him more of a suspect, or less.

And last on my list? Vyviane. A name I hated to put on there but had to.

I hated that I had to make this list at all. These people may have not been my friends, exactly, but they were all people I had known a long time. People whose lives had woven in and around mine.

But I had a feeling there was someone I was missing, too.

Money. I underlined the word in my notebook.

Roderick was pissed that he thought I was taking business from him. A business I didn't even know he had. Did he have investors breathing down his neck? Or was he a sole proprietor, like me?

I noted the questions down, then moved on.

Sapphire was a show cat. There must be money in that, but how much? For one, it cost a lot to keep a show animal in all the things they needed. But did cat show prizes include money? Or just ribbons?

Add in the fact that Petunia was dead? That made things more complex. Who would benefit from all of this?

Sapphire could have been stolen to take her out of the running by a rival show cat owner. But then, what about Mr. Cheeks and Princess Sparkle Toes? What did they have to do with anything?

Clearly, they were in the thick of it, but I couldn't see why or how.

And Sweetheart? I never trusted him. And he was just the sort of person who was always running an angle. I'm not sure how he makes a living, but he always has plenty of money. Or seems to.

"Some of these people must be in cahoots."

That would account for some of my confusion. Two perpetrators, instead of one. Divvy up responsibility. Lead anyone looking into things on a merry chase.

But who was it? Sweetheart and Vyviane? Roderick and Sparkle Toes? Some other combination? All of the above?

I needed someone who knew animals to make sense of it all.

Pulling out my phone, I texted John.

I'll meet you at Ron's, I said. *Convince him to close early or something. We need to talk through the case.*

I waited. And waited. No answer. I paced the shop, staring out the windows at Pride Street just outside. Our beautiful little hamlet. A place of cherry trees, elms, and maples. A place of bars and restaurants, and a new bookshop.

A place where a gay trans man from rural Oregon could find a home.

A place now down one popular florist. Who would take Petunia's place? Would Flower Frenzy close permanently?

Finally, my phone buzzed in my hand.

Heading to Ron's now to get supplies for Sapphire. Will tell him. Come down when you can.

Be there in ten, I texted back. I began shutting down the computer, closed my notebook, and headed toward the back to wash my mug. That chore done, I was ready to grab my messenger bag and head out. Lost in thought, I did my usual scan of the store, making sure nothing was too out of place so I was ready for the following day.

The bells at the front door chimed.

Standing there was Princess Sparkle Toes.

She looked terrible. Her lipstick was smeared on one corner, her eyes looked as if she hadn't slept in days, her retro purple pantsuit was even wrinkled. And worse? Beneath the red straps of her sandals, her toenail polish was chipped. That meant something was very, very wrong.

I noticed she had her little pink purse that held Mr. Cheeks.

"Sparkle Toes!" I said, keeping my voice light. "I see you found Mr. Cheeks. We were worried he was dead."

She looked startled, as if Mr. Cheeks was the last thing on her mind. "Oh. Yes. He was hiding behind the bathtub, silly thing! Made himself a little nest of toilet paper. That's how I finally found him. I followed some tissue scraps."

"I wish you'd told us. We were worried."

She frowned. "Oh. Sorry. Things have been busy."

"I'm a little busy myself. I'm just heading out. Did you need something in particular?"

Sparkle Toes stepped toward me, positioned so she was blocking the door. She seemed nervous and a little brittle, as if she might burst into tears at any moment. Or explode.

She was also taller than me, and outweighed me, too. I calculated whether or not I could get past her if I needed to. After all, she was wearing heels.

"Sparkle Toes? Are you going to tell me why you're here?"

She licked her painted lips. Queens, I tell you. I love them, but they are fond of the dramatic pause. I'm glad John isn't that way. But then, he's only in drag mode on occasion, and nightclubs aren't his way of life.

That suits me, just fine. I'm a low drama kind of guy.

"You know things," she finally said.

"I know things."

She nodded, then pulled a snub nose gun out from the little pink purse.

"You carry a gun with Mr. Cheeks?" I asked. "What if he accidentally pulls the trigger?"

What the heck? Who puts a gun in their animal carrier with the animal still in there?

"Mr. Cheeks doesn't have enough strength in his paws," she remarked calmly, as if this was an ordinary pet owner to pet owner conversation. "A rat, now, they're stronger. And smarter. A rat could pull a trigger for sure."

She looked at me again. "But not a hamster."

"Forgive me for asking, Princess Sparkle Toes, but why, exactly, are you carrying a gun in your hamster purse?"

And why are you waving it around my store?

And suddenly, she was sobbing.

"You. Your life is so perfect. You and your perfect little dogs, and your perfect handsome husband. And who are you? You're nothing! A nobody!"

She sounded like she'd been talking to Vyviane. And I didn't like it one bit. I squared off my shoulders and stepped toward her, still trying to figure out if I could disarm her.

"What does my being a nobody have to do with anything?" I spoke calmly, approaching as quickly and quietly as I could. Lucky for me, she was still sobbing into her hands.

One of which gripped that tiny little gun.

Close enough.

I grabbed her right wrist with one hand, and wrenching the gun out with the other hand, I pushed her away from me. She stumbled backwards, then fell to the ground.

The little pink plastic purse flew into the air, a frantic looking Mr. Cheeks scrabbling for purchase.

I stumbled a bit, clinging to the gun, but righted myself before crashing into a small occasional table that I'd been meaning to move out of the aisle.

Mr. Cheeks scrambled beneath a chair. Great.

Princess Sparkle Toes sat, long legs splayed out, crying as if her heart would burst.

Did I mention I preferred a quiet life?

Eyes still on Sparkle Toes, I texted John.

There's been a change in plans…

CHAPTER 27
Marsha

WE RAN to the store as fast as we could and burst through the door.

Sparkle Toes was slumped on the floor in the aisle and Garrett looked distressed.

I growled at Sparkle Toes as John rushed by me.

"Where's the gun?" John asked, grabbing Garrett's shoulders as if he was going to shake him or pull him into the biggest hug of his life.

"My pocket," Garrett said. "I didn't want to turn my back on Sparkle Toes."

"I've got her," Ron said.

"*Me, too,*" Fred woofed. The black lab was half sitting on Princess Sparkle Toes as Klaus and I swarmed around her. She wasn't going anywhere.

"Let's get that locked up, okay babe?"

John led Garrett to the back.

"*Did you hear that?*" Klaus asked.

"*Hear what?*"

Then I did. Squeaking, like someone was opening and shutting a tiny door.

"Mr. Cheeks!" I barked. *"Where are you?"*

Klaus and I began sniffing around. The hamster couldn't have gone very far.

"Let's get you into a chair," Ron said to the sobbing Sparkle Toes. I swear, things were getting weirder and weirder.

As I sniffed behind sofas, sideboards, and chairs, I had a thought.

"Hey, Fred."

"Yes?" The black lab strolled over.

"Did Ron ever see that bicycle again? Or did you?"

Fred sadly shook his head. *"No. No bicycles with cat carriers, at any rate. We see a lot of bicycles around, though."*

He was right. People in this neighborhood even bike in the rain. I bet Xavier had a bicycle. Which reminded me…

"Any news on Sapphire?"

"She got to Leo's just fine. He said he'll take care of her and let the man and younger man know when she's ready."

Klaus yipped in discovery. *"Mr. Cheeks! Come out! It's safe now!"*

Bright, beady little eyes peered out from beneath a cozy chair, whiskers quivering.

"I don't believe you," Mr. Cheeks moaned. *"My life has been a living hell. One frightening thing after another has happened to me. I can't even begin to tell you…"*

Except he was about to. Once that hamster started talking, there was no way to shut him up.

"Mr. Cheeks," I interrupted. *"Why did I think you were dead? Your cage smelled funny."*

"Oh!" He actually waddled out, puffing up his little white chest. Mr. Cheeks is tan and white and looks like Klaus. If Klaus were a hamster. *"Some Bad People were sniffing around and being mean to Sparkle Toes. A man and a woman. They threatened to take me away if she didn't do what they said. So, I buried a piece of ham I stole from the kitchen counter in my sawdust and paper curls. If they thought I was dead, they wouldn't take me."*

He looked at me. *"It worked? The ham stunk up my cage like I was dead?"*

Mr. Cheeks looked so proud.

"Yes, Mr. Cheeks. Well done. But then, how did you get out of your cage?"

He gripped the carpet with his little claws and walked closer. I could hear Princess Sparkle Toes wailing, and Ron saying some soothing words, but I focused on the hamster. This was more important.

"That one—" he jerked his fuzzy tiny head toward the wailing noises *"—was upset and drank too much of that nasty stuff humans seem to like. When she put me in my cage, she didn't lock it. So, I got out and hid. Easy peasy."*

I looked at Klaus, who looked back at me.

"Then why did she call Garrett?"

"Oh," Mr. Cheeks replied, *"she really thought I was missing. I wasn't sure it was safe to come out, but I finally did when I saw how upset she was. Besides, I got hungry."*

I could respect that.

Garrett and John came back, carrying trays with cups of tea and glasses of water for all the humans, and a pile of what I hoped were treats for us.

"Come on, Mr. Cheeks. Treats!"

The little hamster waddled his way toward the humans as fast as he could. I valiantly stayed back and walked slowly, while Klaus raced ahead, nose intent on the treats. The little pig.

Once the humans all had drinks and the animals had our treats, John leaned toward Princess Sparkle Toes.

"You pulled a gun on my husband," he said.

"John." Garrett put a hand on his arm, but John just shook his head.

"She needs to tell us why." When John got that tone in his voice, it meant you better listen. Klaus and I had learned that the hard way.

Sparkle Toes wiped her face on one of Garrett's handkerchiefs. Most of her makeup was gone and she looked sad, and a little bit like Sapphire had when we found her.

"They've been threatening me. And Mr. Cheeks. And they think Garrett knows too much."

"Knows too much about what?" Ron asked. He sounded as confused as I felt.

"About the fixed cat competitions."

I was horrified.

"*Klaus!*" I barked. "*They fix all the animals before they can compete!*"

"*We're fixed, silly.*"

Oh. I'd forgotten.

"So, let me get this straight," Ron said. His voice was soft, but he sounded angry. "Someone is betting on the cat shows and someone else is fixing the results?"

Sparkle Toe nodded, wadding up the handkerchief in her hands.

"Can you tell us who?"

She burst into tears again.

Oh boy. I went back to chewing my treat. This was going to take a while.

John stood up and clapped his fingers in front of her face.

I yelped, and Fred woofed.

"Sparkle Toes! Snap out of it! You do not get to come in here, wave a gun around, collapse on the floor, and then not tell us what is going on. Tell me now. Who. Is. Threatening. My. Husband?"

CHAPTER 28
Garrett

MY HEART SWELLED inside my chest. I was so filled with love for John in that moment.

Never in my life had I felt so loved and protected. Not before I met him. And to see him like this? I fell in love all over again. Harder and deeper than when I fell the first time.

But I was also confused. I had most definitely not put two and two together about Sapphire missing—other than she herself might be worth money—and corruption at the cat shows, so I didn't see why someone thought I had.

I mean, if all a cat won was a blue ribbon, there would be no need for the fuss. Unless you were breeding the cat, or using it for advertising maybe, a ribbon was just a ribbon, no matter what the color was.

If Ron was right, though, it started to make sense. If people were bribing judges and betting on winners? That meant, despite no purse, there was big money in those competitions. And more drama than the stage at Enrico's club.

"At first, I thought it was Vyviane," Princess Sparkle

Toes said, "because she came to visit and was nosing around. But now I don't think so anymore. It was Sweetheart Digs. And some cronies. I don't know who they are."

Well. And didn't that just add up neatly?

Princess Sparkle Toes was spilling all the tea now. Guess she just needed that little breakdown first. I just wish that hadn't included waving a gun in my face.

"I should have known," John muttered. Right. I think we were going to have that talk about him and Sweetheart sometime soon.

"Do we actually think he killed Petunia?" I asked.

It was hard to tell what people like Sweetheart Digs were capable of. He covered anything real with his *I'm a good guy who helps everybody and likes to party* veneer, so I had no idea what he was really like inside.

Some people say that anyone is capable of murder, but I'm not so sure about that. I think it takes a special sort of ego or a massive stockpile of resentment or fear to murder someone. Or maybe I'm just naive and everyone has a murderous impulse lurking somewhere deep inside.

But if that's the case? I'd rather be naive than think the worst of people. I'll leave that to my thriller and mystery writer husband. John has enough cynicism for the both of us. But he also has a lot of heart. That's why his books sell so well, I guess. It's a winning combination.

As I looked around our little circle, I noticed no one had answered my question.

Princess Sparkle Toes was staring into her mug of tea is if her life depended on it. She was probably ashamed she'd threatened to shoot me, and was scared John was going to yell at her again. That was good, I guess. But right now? I needed answers.

"Sparkle Toes."

She flinched.

"Sparkle Toes. Look at me."

She slowly raised her eyes to meet mine, but she kept blinking, false eyelashes like demented spiders bobbing up and down. She also wouldn't meet my eyes for long. They kept darting side to side. As someone who can have trouble with eye contact, I get it. But it was kind of annoying.

"You have to tell us everything you know. If people are threatening you, and sent you to threaten me, that's serious."

"Plus, someone stole Sapphire," Ron pointed out. "That's pretty bad, too."

None of us mentioned that Sapphire was safe, I noticed. Sparkle Toes may be crying on my couch, but that didn't mean she was trustworthy.

"I feel terrible about that," she whispered. "But you don't understand how much money is riding on this show."

"How many people are involved?" John asked.

Sparkle Toes shrugged. "Half a dozen?"

"Why did they kill Petunia?" I asked.

She shook her head.

"That's what I don't understand. It was never part of the plan." Sparkle Toes stared into her tea again, as if seeking answers. Or maybe courage. "I mean, not that I know of. They don't tell me half of it, I'm sure. But Petunia wasn't supposed to die! They just wanted Sapphire out of commission for the big show this weekend. One of the judges really favors her, and they want some other cat to win."

"But Petunia is dead," John said. "That's a fact. Died from a blow to the head."

"Which she probably got from falling!" Sparkle Toes burst out. "Sweetheart was going to get information from her. They must have gotten into a fight, and she fell! You know how those two were. He wouldn't kill her!"

I was so confused. "No, Sparkle Toes, I have no idea how those two were. Are you telling me they were lovers or something? Or did they have a history together?"

My eyes darted to John when I said that. I couldn't help it. He flushed but didn't look away. I released a sigh.

"And why go fight with Petunia at all? With Sapphire already out of the way, what did he need to confront her about?"

Sparkle Toes suddenly set her tea down and stood.

"You're not going anywhere," Ron said, voice mild.

"Fine!" she snapped. "I just need to move. I can't sit still anymore!"

"Because you feel guilty about something?" John asked. His voice was also mild, but I knew he was still seething.

"I do! I do feel guilty! Petunia was my friend!" She whirled on me. "If you hadn't started investigating, everything would have been fine! Or maybe not…"

She was blaming me for this mess?

"What do you mean?" I felt like I was holding my breath.

"Sweetheart went to confront Petunia because he thought you'd helped her get her damn cat back! Sapphire disappeared, and we couldn't be sure she wasn't holed up somewhere, prepping for the big show in secret! It would have ruined all of Sweetheart's plans. His people were getting antsy."

"Wait a minute," John said. "You said 'we' couldn't be

sure. I'm still not exactly clear what your role in all of this was."

Sparkle Toes went back to pacing, wringing her hands, pink fingernails flashing like flamingos ready to take flight.

"Sweetheart Digs knew I had money trouble. He told me if I helped distract Petunia, and then kept you from investigating, he would help me out once the bets were counted and the payday came through. I was supposed to keep Sapphire in the safe house, but Sweetheart got paranoid and wanted her moved."

"It was you on the bicycle," Ron said. "You're the one I saw."

She stopped then, head held in her hands, and started sobbing.

"Oh, snap out of it!" John said. "You made a mess of this bed, and now you have to wash the sheets and remake it!"

Nice metaphor. I think.

"But..." Even with some puzzle pieces slotting into place, I was still confused. "If you were in the middle of all of this, why in the world did you call me about Mr. Cheeks?"

She looked up at me, tears streaming in deep grooves down what makeup was left on her face.

"Because I love Mr. Cheeks. I was desperate. He's my only real friend. Even Petunia... Let's just say after she started dating Sweetheart Digs in secret, our friendship cooled."

Well. That I could understand. If one of my friends was dating the self-proclaimed Mayor of Pride Street, I probably wouldn't want to hang out with them much, either.

"And then Sapphire escaped, and you couldn't find

her, and Sweetheart was convinced she'd made her way back home to Petunia, who was keeping her under lock and key until the show."

And then they fought about it. And now Petunia was dead. It was so unnecessary and foolish, it made me queasy.

"When is the show?" Ron chimed in.

I sent him a grateful look for keeping us on track. I was also grateful that the dogs had been quiet this whole time. That's what comes of giving out treats that require intensive chewing.

"Today is Friday?" Sparkle Toes asked, then tapped a pink fingernail against her lips. "Contestants start checking in tonight. Any time after five pm. Doors open to the public tomorrow morning at nine."

"Ron?" I asked. "Are you willing to close up shop tomorrow?"

"If I have to," he said. "I mean, Saturday's my big sales day, so it's not the greatest, but you know what? I never take a vacay, either. What's the plan?"

"We're going to a cat show."

CHAPTER 29

Marsha

I DIDN'T LIKE BEING in this little duffle bag. Not one bit. It was undignified. I didn't care about the ventilation holes, or the screened portion I could look out of. A corgi is meant to see and be seen!

Klaus willingly went along—and got praised for it, the stinker—but he was probably just happy to have a nice place to take a nap until show time.

Ron rigged up some sort of harness for Fred and was calling him an emotional support dog. Garrett and John argued about that, Garrett saying it was unethical, and John saying it was no worse than smuggling two corgis in using carrying bags.

So here we were, inside the arena.

"Your dog must stay on leash at all times!"

Uh oh. Trouble. I peered through the mesh screen. A woman in a blue suit with the clipboard next to the registration desk looked flustered.

"I understand that," Ron said. "Fred is good with cats and is very well behaved."

"Well, keep him close," she snapped. "At all times!"

"Gotcha." I heard the smile in Ron's voice. "Now, may we pay?"

She nodded, but I could tell she didn't want to.

"Very irregular," she muttered as Ron and John handed over credit cards, and then we were in, walking across an expanse of ugly, swirling carpet and through a sea of people talking too loudly.

"*You think Garrett got in okay?*" I woofed softly, hoping Klaus was awake.

"*I hope so,*" he barked back.

Several heads turned our way, and people frowned, staring at Fred.

"*I guess a cat show really isn't the best place for dogs. These people don't look very friendly.*" I kept my barks soft.

"*I don't see why,*" Fred remarked. He kept his eyes trained straight ahead though, so as not to draw attention to our bags. "*I like cats just fine. Don't you?*"

"*Some cats,*" I said.

I sniffed. We must be heading toward toward the food carts, where Ron and John both stopped for coffee.

"I'm gonna need more caffeine to get through this day," John muttered. "I hope Garrett knows what he's doing."

I was worried, too. The plan sounded very complicated to me. I'd even asked Adam about it last night. The ghost had said it sounded like a blast, and he wished he could be there with us to take the bad people down.

But he didn't call them bad people. He used a different word that I won't repeat.

Then John, Fred, and Ron followed the crowd to an enormous, echoey room. I pressed an eye against my mesh screen, straining to see. The edges of the space were filled with tables and all things cat.

"There's Roderick!" I barked.

"Roderick! Roderick!" Klaus barked.

More people stared.

"Ssh!" John hissed. Uh oh. We probably shouldn't be barking, but how else were we supposed to communicate?

Roderick looked up from where he was arranging a display of cute collars. He looked startled.

"He looks spooked," John said.

"Didn't Garrett tell him we'd be here?" Ron asked.

"I thought so. Should we go talk to him, or pretend we don't know each other?"

I think there were parts of the plan that didn't get worked out so well, but then, I'm just a corgi. What do I know about plans?

"I think the barking duffle bags already blew our cover in that regard," Ron said, and started walking that way, skirting clumps of people cooing over cat toys and little knitted hats that I'm sure their cats were mortified to have put on their heads.

But I did want to have a look at Roderick's new collar collection. I'd overheard him saying he was launching it here. Whatever that means. I thought the word launch was for frisbees or other flying objects. As far as I could tell, dog collars didn't fly.

"Hey, Roderick," John greeted the man, who looked very nervous, then unzipped my duffle so I could poke my head out. Sweet relief!

Roderick pushed his glasses up his nose and wiped his palms on his dark jeans.

I found the air in the conference center to be pleasant. When you wear a fur coat, cool air is always welcome. But Roderick was sweating.

"Uh. Hi. You guys came."

"He doesn't sound happy about seeing us," Klaus yipped. His nose just crested the zipper of his duffle.

"That's because he's not," Fred replied.

All of a sudden, I wished Bruiser was here, but Garrett said Bex and Jacki couldn't close the café on a Saturday or their customers would riot. Sounds extreme to me, but then, I don't drink coffee. Besides, Bruiser didn't much like cats.

And no way would he fit inside a bag.

"Didn't Garrett tell you we'd be here?" Ron asked, leaning over the counter, as Fred nosed at some sparkly bows.

"You think I could wear one of these?" the old lab asked me.

I peered down at the table. Being this high was interesting.

"Why not? A little bling never hurt anybody."

Fred barked at Ron.

"You like these, huh? Okay. Which one? Blue? That'll really pop against your black fur."

Ron bought Fred a sparkly blue bow tie and snugged it around his neck. Fred looked happier than I'd seen him. Ever. Turns out the way to his heart is fancy canine wear.

"Where's Garrett then?" Roderick asked.

"In the staging area, we hope. You still good to play your part?" John asked.

Roderick looked around, then licked his lips and nodded.

"Yeah. I've got everything ready. Just in case. But frankly? I hope I don't need to be involved."

If you ask me, Roderick looked like he was about to be sick again. John gave him a look, the kind he got when he was about to start in on a long conversation.

"Let's go find Garrett!" I barked, just as an announcer-voice came over the loudspeaker.

"The first round begins in five minutes. Rings two, four, and six. If you wish to attend, please take a seat in the arena."

"Come on, doggos," Ron said. "Let's go check out some fancy cats."

I guessed finding Garrett would have to wait. I just hoped he was okay.

CHAPTER 30

Garrett

MY BOUQUET WAS RIDICULOUS, but it was the only way I could think of to disguise myself without actually wearing a disguise.

John, Sparkle Toes, and I had snuck into Flower Frenzy way too early. And by snuck in, I mean broke in. It was weird being inside the shop without Petunia, and weirder still seeing the streaks of black powder everywhere the cops had dusted for fingerprints.

They hadn't found anything unusual and were calling it an accidental slip and fall. Who they expected to clean up the mess, I didn't know. I also didn't know what was going to happen to the shop. If I had the money, I would buy it and hire someone to run it myself, but I just don't have that kind of cash.

At any rate, there were enough decent looking flowers left in the cooler to cobble together an impressive bouquet that would cover my face and also get me into the staging area where the cats, trainers, and groomers prepped for show.

All I had to do was say delivery, make up a cat's name,

and the harried, overworked person at the back door let me in with a roll of their eyes.

Peeking past the ridiculous array of mums, gladiolus, and a bunch of other flowers whose names I couldn't begin to tell you, I scanned the big, brightly lit space for Xavier, Charles, and Sapphire.

Behind a row of tall, curtained dividers, there were cats in cages everywhere. Each little cat area was curtained, too. Guess you didn't want the cats checking out the competition.

Or clawing each other's eyes out.

There were cats getting brushed. Cats getting bows. Cats getting massages. Cats yowling. Cats purring. And in the midst of it all, humans. Also everywhere. Shrieking, and rushing, and sniping. Grabbing combs. Stealing towels.

Despite the separation between cages, it really reminded me of the dressing room at Enrico's, the few times John had actually performed. Yikes.

Finally, my eyes lighted on the one calm space in the bustling room. There was Charles, sitting in a folding chair, hands on his cane, calm as you please. His white hair looked neatly arranged on top of his head, and he was chatting with Xavier, who was attempting to attach a bow to Sapphire's head. Sapphire looked calm, too, which was amazing considering the clamor going on, and the ordeal she'd recently been subjected to. I guess some proper treatment at Leo's Grooming Palace and a few days of peace under Charles's and Xavier's care had done the trick.

Or maybe she was a true professional.

I made my way toward the two men, using the flowers to block my face as much as I could without running into anyone or anything. Maybe acting as a florist was foolish, but it was the best way I could think of to get staging area access at short notice.

It also felt as if I was carrying a bit of Petunia with me. She deserved to be in on this, even if she was dead.

"Delivery for Princess Sapphire of the Flowing Silver Locks," I said, stepping up to the table.

Xavier smirked. "That's not her registered name, you know."

I waved him off and set down the bouquet. "Everything going okay here? Has anyone been by to harass you?"

Xavier got Sapphire settled back in her well-cushioned enclosure.

Charles coughed. "Other than a couple of snooty white women who were just sure this *could not be our cat, could it*?" He mimicked a high pitched, arrogant voice. "Because no way would two Black men be able to afford a cat like Sapphire, let alone the grooming and entry fees and all the rest."

"Yeah," Xavier agreed. "And we've gotten some looks. But you were right, as long as we had Sapphire's paperwork, we were good to go."

People. I swear. Just because some of them were dripping in money didn't mean they weren't small-minded bigots. As a matter of fact, sometimes money just made them worse, because their bigotry was compounded by a sense of entitlement.

"Sorry you're having to deal with that."

"Garrett, in all my years of living as a gay Black man in a seventy-five percent white town? I've seen pretty much everything. If you don't learn to roll with it, misery dogs your heels every day."

"That doesn't make it right, old man," Xavier said, voice quiet.

"No," I agreed. "It doesn't."

I scanned the maelstrom again, even though I wasn't sure exactly what I was looking for. Would Sweetheart and his henchmen—henchpeople?—be back here, or in the stands? That was the question of the hour, and the reason Ron and John were out front, while Xavier, Charles, and I were back here.

Roderick was also prepared to help, though I didn't trust him and hoped we wouldn't need him.

"You seen Sweetheart Digs yet?" I asked.

"That guy," Xavier muttered. "I saw him walk by, but he was all the way across the room and didn't see us. But his people could've come through and we might not have known it."

That made sense. I wondered if Sweetheart had clocked Sapphire's presence yet, and what his response would be. All I knew was, I hoped us being here tripped him up. Made him confess to his crimes.

Or maybe I'd just been reading too many of John's books.

Xavier reached into the enclosure and gently stroked Sapphire's lustrous gray fur. She gazed up at him adoringly and purred.

"Seems like you two are getting along," I remarked.

"Oh. Yeah. Now that she knows she's safe, Sapphire's great." Xavier's smile was a little bit dreamy, as if he'd just met the boy or girl he'd been waiting for. Cute.

Charles chuckled. "Those two are in lo-ove."

"Hush!" Xavier said, then trained his dark eyes on me. "I think Petunia was a bit high strung and made Sapphire nervous. At least, that's what Leo said. I mean, look at how happy she is. All these other cats looked stressed the eff out."

I saw what he meant. The people were certainly stressed, and that would rub off on their pets. Animals are sensitive to human mood changes and act accordingly. And now that I knew what a high stakes game some of these people were playing?

Let's just say I'd probably be stressed out, too.

"Well, now that I've delivered Sapphire's flowers, I'm going to wander. See if I can flush out Sweetheart Digs. Or eavesdrop on some cat related drama."

"Plenty of that around these parts." Charles rolled his eyes. "You go on. But you've got that man of yours on speed dial, don't you? And you have Xavier's number, too?"

I patted the pocket that held my phone. "Safe and sound."

Though whether my phone would work in this concrete hall was anyone's guess.

Time to do some reconnaissance, then get this ball rolling.

It was time to take Sweetheart Digs down.

And hope I didn't get kicked out of the arena in the process.

CHAPTER 31

Marsha

THE SHOW WAS FASCINATING. At first. Then it got kind of boring. They'd let us out of our duffle bags, but we still weren't allowed to run around and sniff at things.

"Keep your ears on a swivel," I said to Klaus. *"And use your eyes, too."*

We shared a seat between Ron and John, with poor Fred squeezed on the floor in front of us. The old lab sat up, but his view was blocked by the person in the row in front of ours.

"I can't see anything," he moaned. *"And this person stinks."*

They did, too. The acrid scent of cologne and hairspray tickled my nose and made it hard to smell anything else. And my nose wasn't an inch from the person's blonde head, like Fred's.

Meanwhile, down at the bottom of the big arena, I had thought the cats would be doing tricks or something. But no. They just walked around and posed on tables in three different rings while a judge held up their tails and other things that looked pretty undignified to me.

"I thought there would be skill and agility tests," I complained. *"Who wants to watch a bunch of cats pose and get measured?"*

"All these people," Fred said, finally giving up with a sigh and easing his older bones to the floor.

He was right. All these people. And we weren't here to watch the cats, anyway. We were looking for that man they called Sweetheart. Though he never seemed like such a Sweetheart to me.

I listened for his too loud voice, and looked for a flash of silver. He loved anything silvery and sparkly.

"Do you see him?" John leaned across us and asked Ron. He patted my head absently. He also blocked my view.

So, I looked at Ron instead. The big man turned his head this way and that, the long coils of his hair falling over one shoulder. He had a cartoon cat on the T-shirt stretched over his chest and belly today, worn beneath a short sleeve white shirt. The cat was kind of cute, I had to admit. I wondered if he'd gotten the shirt from Roderick.

He shook his head. "I don't. Don't hear him, either. But it's hard to hear anything over the announcer."

The person in front of my seat turned, a scowl on her face.

"Shhh! Some of us are trying to listen!"

"Sorry," Ron said.

The person turned around again.

As she did, I saw a flash of silver heading to a pair of double doors.

I barked. *"It's him!"*

"Where?" Klaus asked, as Fred scrambled back up to his feet.

"There!" I turned to John. *"It's him!"*

Both John and Ron's heads snapped toward where my nose was pointed. They gathered up our leashes.

"Control your mutts!" the person said. "Or I'm calling security! Of all things, bringing dogs to a cat show…"

I snapped at her but didn't lunge or anything. Though I wanted to.

"Your dog just tried to bite me!" she shrieked, rising from her chair.

"Sorry ma'am," John said, lips tight. "We're leaving."

"Good!" she sniffed and sat back down.

"Hurry!" I barked. *"He's getting away!"*

CHAPTER 32
Garrett

I WAS ROUNDING one of the long aisles, looking for anything helpful, when two of the royal blue curtains separating the staging area from the rest of the arena swept open and in walked Sweetheart Digs, followed by a man and a woman I didn't recognize. They didn't look like Pride Street people, if you know what I mean.

They wore boring suits, navy on the man and pearl gray on the woman. Sweetheart was in his usual silver lamé jacket, those stupid sunglasses propped on top of his head, diamond studs winking in the harsh white lights.

I moved, trying to dodge behind a tall, gangly man carrying a Siamese in a cage.

But Sweetheart's blue eyes caught me, piercing me as if I was a mouse, caught in his claws.

He scowled, then wiped his face, then smiled and headed toward me. I swear, that man is creepy. It was like watching Linda Blair in the Exorcist coming toward me, if Linda Blair wore hundred-dollar silk and bamboo T-shirts, and was a gay man walking on two feet, instead of crawling backwards down the stairs.

Gah! My brain was getting overwhelmed by the lights and sounds and too many people. Why hadn't I had John do this part of the job? I couldn't do this.

::You can.::

"Adam?" I could swear I'd heard a ghostly voice in my head, one I thought I'd imagined at our house. I ran nervous fingers over the wide silver band that used to belong to Adam, but the ghost didn't say anything more.

But his voice had helped, anyway. I breathed deeply, smelling cats, and pee, and grooming products. I planted my Oxford shoes on the linoleum covered floor.

Then, giving Adam's ring one more swipe for luck, I squared my shoulders and faced down Sweetheart Digs.

Suddenly, Xavier was standing shoulder to shoulder with me. Or really, his shoulders were much higher than mine, but you get the point.

"You got this," he said. But I noticed he kept his hands loose at his sides, ready to strike if necessary.

"You trained in self-defense or something?" I asked out of the side of my mouth.

Sweetheart Digs' progress had been slowed by clusters of people stopping him to talk. His eyes kept darting my way, as if willing me to stay put.

"You might say I have," Xavier replied. "Seven years of Aikido and three of regular self-defense."

Sounded like a useful combination.

"Xavier," I said, risking taking my eyes off Sweetheart for a moment, "I'm glad to have you at my side."

He smiled down at me with warm brown eyes.

"Glad to be here. I hate people who mess with animals. It isn't right."

When I looked back, Sweetheart Digs wasn't there

anymore, and John, Ron, and the dogs came barreling through the curtains.

Klaus barked at me and tugged on his leash, but Marsha tugged the opposite direction. John saw me, waved, then pointed and hurried after Marsha, who was leaping like a tiny sled dog down the center aisle.

"Oh no," Xavier said.

"What? What's happening?" I started moving toward John, but Xavier stopped me.

"We can cut him off at the pass. Come on!"

"Wait? What?"

But Xavier was already loping down the aisle on those long legs of his. And all of a sudden, I saw the flash of silver lame.

Sweetheart Digs was heading for Sapphire. And Charles.

Xavier and I both started to run. Watching his narrow back weave and bob between frantic, high-strung people and their cats was like watching poetry. I put on a burst of speed, already panting, trying to keep up with my shorter legs and my I don't do cardio lungs.

He leapt over an empty cat crate sticking out into the aisle and turned a corner. I narrowly avoided bashing into the crate with my shins, caught myself on the corner of a table. A Persian cat swiped at my hand but missed.

I turned the corner just as Xavier reached the booth where Charles sat, clutching Sapphire to his chest, with Sweetheart Digs yelling and grabbing at the hissing cat. John and Ron were pounding up the aisle.

"You!" Sweetheart Digs was screaming. His white face was flushed red, and spittle flew from his mouth. Charles turned his head to avoid the spray, but his hands gripped Sapphire, hard.

The cat yowled, hissed, and screamed.

John and Xavier grabbed Sweetheart Digs by the shoulders, but the silver lamé must have been slippery because they couldn't seem to get a grip.

I leaned in, trying to get between Sweetheart and Charles.

"Sweetheart!" I yelled. "Stop it!"

I heard what must have been show security bellowing behind us.

And then Ron leaned in, shoving his body against Sweetheart Digs and grasping his wrists.

"Let go of the cat." Ron's voice was like ice, cutting through the clamor. I'd never heard the mild-mannered man sound like that before.

"Piss off!" Sweetheart spat. "You don't know what you're involved in."

Show security was trying to get through the small crowd now gathered around the booth. Klaus and Marsha barked their heads off, adding to the confusion.

What should I do?

::Look for a way through.::

Adam's voice—it *must* be him—steadied me. He was right. This was where being small had an advantage. I angled my shoulders sideways and pushed my way through a minuscule crack between two bodies. I just kept moving and pushing, then formed my hands into a triangle shape that I used as a wedge to help ease me through.

Finally, I popped out from between two shouting people, ducked beneath Ron's big arms, and scooped Sapphire out from the melee. Charles looked surprised but let go as soon as he saw what I was doing. Sweetheart stumbled and fell into Ron, just as two guys in security vests crashed through and hoisted Sweetheart Digs under both arms, practically lifting him through the crowd.

"*Mew?*" Sapphire asked.

"Mew, indeed," I replied. She licked my chin, just one brief swipe, which was Sapphire speak for *I will adore you forever for saving me*, I guess.

And then Klaus, Marsha, and Fred were swarming my feet, John's arms were around me, and Xavier was clapping me on the back.

"Nice work, young men," Charles said. "That was more excitement than I've had in quite a while."

He coughed, and Xavier rooted beneath the table, coming out with a water bottle.

I needed some water myself. And a shower. And a huge meal.

And then I needed to collapse.

CHAPTER 33

Marsha

GARRETT AND JOHN spoked rapidly to two women in black suits as the security guards led Sweetheart Digs away. They gestured toward the man in navy and the woman in pearl gray who were scurrying away.

Two security guards stopped them at the arena doors.

"We did it!" I barked.

"We did it! We did it!" Klaus bounced and pranced, shaking his fuzzy white butt, tail swishing with excitement.

"Woof," Fred said. Sometimes a dog just has to woof. Kind of like humans have to say hooray.

"I don't know why you three are so pleased with yourselves," Sapphire meowed. She was safely back in Charles's arms, and the old man didn't look like he was going to let her go. *"I was the one fighting for my life."*

"Well, we caused a distraction, didn't we? And helped Garrett get you away."

"Yeah," Klaus barked. *"Everyone helped!"*

Sapphire made a noise in her throat, then closed her

eyes and snuggled into Charles's chest. He stroked her gray fur.

Then the announcer came over the loudspeaker. "Princess Sapphire, you are on in five minutes."

Sapphire stretched and blinked.

"What about it, baby girl," Charles asked. "You ready to compete?"

Sapphire leapt lightly from his arms, onto the table.

"I guess that means yes." Charles chuckled, opening her crate. She hopped in, and Xavier picked up the cage hurried off, Charles moving behind him at a fairly rapid clip, considering his cane.

Garrett looked stunned. I pressed up against his legs, offering comfort.

"Thanks, Marsha P." He bent to pat my head.

John handed him and Ron some bottled water, then poured some in Sapphire's dish and set it on the floor for the rest of us to share.

We took turns lapping at the bowl. Sapphire was going to be pissed when she smelled us all over her things.

Too bad, cat.

"Well," Ron asked, "shall we go watch Sapphire do her thing?"

"*Yes!*" I barked.

The cat show might be boring, but it's different when its someone you know.

Unfortunately, heading back to the arena meant getting stuffed back in that darned bag.

Woof.

CHAPTER 34

Garrett

"SO," I asked, as John and I got changed for bed. "You ever going to tell me what went down between you and Sweetheart Digs?"

I slipped Adam's ring from my finger and set it on the dresser in front of his photo. *Thank you*, I thought, and swore I felt a cold tingle on my hand in response.

I felt John pause behind me and turned as he drew his favorite anime sleep shirt on over his head. He never wore it out in public, saying it wasn't fitting for a thriller author to like anime, but he liked wearing it to bed. He's so cute.

"Sweetheart?" he asked, then sat on the edge of the bed in loose cotton pants and that candy colored shirt. He patted the comforter, inviting me to join him.

I sat down and crossed my legs beneath me, then snuggled up into his side. He put an arm around my waist. It felt good. Right. No matter what he had to tell me, in this moment? We were fine.

"Sweetheart Digs was one of the first people I met when I moved here. He was bright, and generous, and funny. At least I thought so. I fell under his spell."

John's voice was tinged with regret. "I fell under his spell like I was a wide-eyed twenty-year-old from the sticks."

"Like I was, you mean?"

He gave me a squeeze but ignored my words.

"I thought I was in love. But then I saw that he was using me. Using everyone around him. So, I finally wised up and left. He was angry and tried to turn people against me for a while. Some people believed him. But then he turned on them, too."

I kissed his shoulder. "And now?"

"Well, you see why I despise the man. But that's why I ended up with some of the friends we have. They rallied around me."

"And why didn't you ever tell me this?"

I felt him shrug.

"By the time we met, I was on an even keel again. It just didn't seem important. I didn't want to give that man another ounce of my attention."

I exhaled. "Well, he forced us to pay attention this time, didn't he?"

We both sat for a time, just breathing together, listening to the dogs snore. I thought I felt Adam moving around the room, but that might have been my imagination.

"Well," I said, breaking the silence. "He'll get some of what's coming to him, now. There's no proof he killed Petunia, but organized betting, and rigging cat shows? A little bird told me they've been gathering evidence for the past two years. The cat show people already stripped his credentials, and it sounds like their forensic accountants are hard at work, trying to figure out how much money is at play and exactly how many people are involved."

"Well," John said. "That might not exactly be justice, but at least it's something."

"At least it's something," I agreed. Then I pulled my husband down on the bed. He kissed me, and all thoughts of cat shows and dastardly fake mayors drifted away.

CHAPTER 35

Adam

I LISTENED to the sounds of the house, settling around me. The dogs snored in their big bed in John and Garrett's room upstairs.

The men kissed and talked softly in the big bed outside my closet, in one of those moments that long-term partners shared.

I floated into the room. I was getting used to not really walking now. Though my boots still moved in the old, familiar way, there was no thumping and creaking on the hundred plus year old wood.

My ring winked from the dresser top, amongst keys and other jewelry and the photo of me that Garrett had pulled from the box and framed.

It was the picture of me getting my community service award for all the work I did with ACT UP and the local hospice. I wore a crisp white shirt under my leather vest, but my boots and leather pants and cap shone, as if I was going to a club. Those well-cared-for leathers were part of who I am.

Or who I was.

I wasn't sure who I was right now, but the dogs? They provided comfort.

And Garrett wearing my ring meaning I could talk to him somehow? Well, that was something new, wasn't it? A thing to learn and practice.

I always liked learning new things when I was alive. And one thing I learned? No matter how good some people have it, they'll always choose greed over community.

I'd known plenty of people like Sweetheart Digs. But luckily, I'd known a lot more like Ron, Garrett, and John.

Good people are everywhere, trying to do the right thing.

And that helped my spirit rest a bit easier than it otherwise might.

"*Adam?*" Marsha woofed softly as Klaus kept snoring away. "*You okay?*"

::*I'm just fine, Marsha P. Johnson. But thanks. Go back to sleep now.*::

I listened as she settled in and realized my words were true.

"'*Kay. But Adam?*" Marsha's voice was sleepy, and I could tell she was drifting off again. "*We're going to find your dog, me and Klaus. Bring her home.*"

I smiled at the thought. Lucy or no Lucy, I really was fine. And things on Pride Street just might be okay for a while.

THERE'S nothing like a good muffin in the morning. But when the baked goods are laced with murder? A corgi is better off getting treats somewhere else…

Find out what happens next, in *Muffin Murder*!

And more...

If you enjoyed this book, please consider telling a friend, or leaving a short review at your favorite booksellers. Many thanks!

And visit thorncoyle.com to sign up for a weekly newsletter. You can also purchase books direct from author at thorncoylebooks.com

Acknowledgments

A big thank you and yip, yip, hurrah to my Kickstarter backers! Thanks also to my Patreon supporters who were the first to read about Marsha, Klaus, and Adam the ghost. I'm eternally grateful for your support!

Thank you to Bonnie and Jack for reading, to Annie for editing, and to Morpheus and Juniper the Corgi for sharing their corgi expertise. And always, to my chosen family for your years of support.

Most of all, thank you to everyone who fell in love with two men and their dogs and the queer little village-in-a-city they call home.

By Wind

By Sea

By Moon

By Sun

By Dusk

By Dark

By Witch's Mark

The Panther Chronicles (Complete)

To Raise a Clenched Fist to the Sky

To Wrest Our Bodies From the Fire

To Drown This Fury in the Sea

To Stand With Power on This Ground

The Steel Clan Saga

We Seek No Kings

We Heed No Laws

We Ride at Night

Short Story Collections

A Hint of Faery

A Touch of Faery

A Spark of Magic

A Flame for Yuletide

A Hope for Winter

A Time for Magic

A Speculation of Stars

A Speculation of Hope

A Speculation of Time

Risk It All: Queer Stories of Love, Suspense, And Daring

Thresholds: Queer Stories of Love, Suspense, And Daring

Ghost Talker

Cats and Other Creatures

NON-FICTION

You are the Spell

Sigil Magic for Writers, Artists, & Other Creatives

Crafting a Daily Practice

Resistance Matters

Evolutionary Witchcraft

Kissing the Limitless

Make Magic of Your Life

About the Author

T. Thorn Coyle worked in many strange and diverse occupations before settling in to write novels. Buy them a cup of tea and perhaps they'll tell you about it.

Author of the *Seashell Cove Paranormal Cozy Mystery* series, *The Steel Clan Saga*, *The Witches of Portland*, and *The Panther Chronicles*, Thorn's multiple non-fiction books include *Sigil Magic for Writers, Artists & Other Creatives*, and *Evolutionary Witchcraft*.

Thorn's work appears in many anthologies, magazines, and collections. They have taught magical practice in nine countries, on four continents, and in twenty-five states.

An interloper to the Pacific Northwest U.S., Thorn stalks city streets and talks to crows, squirrels, and trees.

Connect with Thorn:
www.thorncoyle.com

9 781946 476401